Pie Crust
&
Peril

ALSO BY LAURA PAULING

Murder with a Slice of Cheesecake
Footprints in the Frosting
Deadly Independence
Frosted on the Ferris Wheel
Fruitcake and Foul Play
Poison in the Pastry
Catered to Death

A Spy Like Me
Heart of an Assassin
Vanishing Point
Twist of Fate

Prom Impossible
Prompossible Plans
Covert Kissing
Secrets & Sabotage

Heist
A Royal Heist

Pie Crust
&
Peril

Laura Pauling

Redpoint Press

Text copyright 2022 Laura Pauling
All rights reserved.

No part of this publication may be reproduced, stored in a retrieval system or transmitted in any form or by any means, electronic, or otherwise, without written permission from the publisher. For information visit www.laurapauling.com

paperback ISBN 13: 97984333170551

Summary: Holly moves to a new town to be with Trent but a murder interrupts their reunion and possibly their future.

Edited by Cindy Davis

for all mystery lovers

1

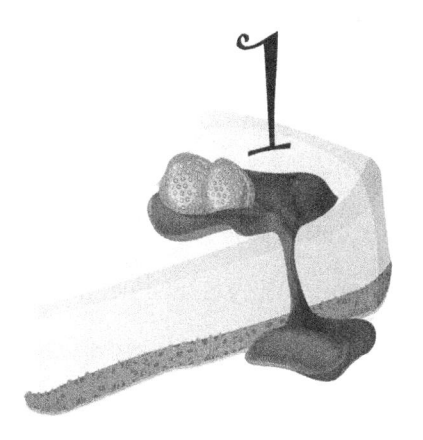

It was overwhelming.

Holly stood outside what used to be her store, *Just Cheesecake*. Now the sign read: *Just Cheesecake & More*. She should feel happy, content, excited. Instead, a feeling of loss and nostalgia stabbed at her heart. She didn't expect this sudden emotion.

Truly, she was opening the door to a new life by walking through this entrance to say goodbye to friends and loved ones. She glanced back at the car, packed and ready to go.

Oh, how she wished Trent could be here. To hold her hand. To whisper in her ear that this was the right decision.

It wasn't like she was moving across the world or something. Bitter sweetness would fall on anyone if they were leaving for Australia or Alaska, but she was moving an hour away. She would still see her friends. And, she would be starting a new chapter of her life with Trent. The diamond on her finger was proof.

"You going to stand there all day in this heat?" Charlene threw out the accusation.

"Maybe." Would her old friend, and Trent's mother, see through her? Of course. "You're supposed to be waiting inside for my surprise going away party."

"Yes, surprise. I never should've told you." Charlene patted her hair. "Now, my hair is wilting, and I'm hankering for some cheesecake."

Holly let out a snort. Charlene could care less about her hair, whether it was frizzy or wilting. Honesty was the best policy. "The memories are overwhelming."

Charlene nudged Holly aside and went to push open the door but paused. In an uncharacteristic moment of empathy, she turned caring eyes on Holly. "I've lived long enough to know that people come and go in your life. That's a fact. Friends are forever, that's true. But they won't always live next door." Then she opened the door and pushed Holly forward.

At first, no one noticed her, which was fine.

It was like she was invisible, staring at a scene from a movie. She blinked back the welling tears. Everyone she loved gathered in one place. Millicent fussed at the food table, arranging platters of mini-cheesecakes, brownies, and cookies. She'd added a bright red streak to her hair to match the new T-shirts of *Just Cheesecake & More*. A large sheet cake sat in the center. Pierre, Millicent's father, leaned on a cane by her side. Various customers and acquaintances were busy talking and nibbling on the sweet treats.

Charlene cleared her throat.

Millicent jerked her head up and gasped. Then she squealed. "She's here! Quick!" As if Holly had arrived early, Millicent rushed through the crowd, handing everyone a party horn.

Everyone cheered and blew into the horns. They gathered around and offered hugs.

After a few minutes, Millicent waved everyone away. "Okay, party girl, you have a special seat." Helium balloons were tied to the top of a chair that sat next to the cake. Millicent patted it. "Here you go."

Holly flashed Charlene a look as if to say *save me*. Charlene smirked. It was just like Millicent to go overboard.

"Shush, everyone. Max?" Millicent's voice made her question more like a command.

"Yes, Miss Millicent." Max grabbed a tray and offered everyone a glass of champagne.

Millicent raised her glass. "A toast. To the best amateur sleuth, after me, of course." Everyone laughed. "Just kidding. Just kidding. To a wonderful friend who has added to this community. We'll all miss her!" She pulled out her phone. Reading from the screen, she said, "Trent sends his wishes and love." She giggled. "And he says, 'Stop stalling and get out here. I miss you!'"

Holly's heart squeezed. She missed him too. He'd moved out early to start his new job as chief of police. He'd been so busy settling in and learning the ropes, they'd barely had two minutes to talk. Never mind spend quality time together. That was one thing to look forward to. Without the drive it would be easier to steal a few moments together.

"Earth to Holly." Millicent waved. "This is where you sip the champagne and burst out crying about how much you'll miss me."

More laughter.

Miss Millicent? Holly had to admit that she would. They'd started out as competitors and frenemies but over the last incident when Teddy tried to force Holly into marriage, they'd had to work together. A friendship had been forged. Holly lifted her glass. "Thank you, everyone." Then her throat closed and she couldn't say much else, even though they stared expectantly.

"How about some cheesecake?" Charlene asked. "Let's eat."

"Thank you," Holly whispered to Charlene when they were in line for treats. "I wasn't up for a speech."

"No problem. You owe me."

With a loaded plate, Holly sat in the seat of honor but found her appetite had disappeared. Instead, she just wanted to soak in this time with cherished friends. Millicent sat to her right, and Charlene to her left. Kitty and Ann sat at the next table over.

"How soon before you're begging us to come help solve a mystery?" Millicent asked with a mouth full of cheesecake. Frosting dotted the corners of her mouth.

"I have a feeling those days are over. I'm not moving to a small town. They have a well-staffed police department." Holly had to admit the truth. "My involvement won't be welcomed."

"Since when has that stopped you?" Charlene retorted.

"Yes, but your boyfriend is the chief, which means you'll have inside access to everything," Millicent persisted. "Files, clues, interviews."

Holly's smile wavered. They'd already had that conversation. Trent had made it clear that his work and their relationship would be separate. That Holly would be so busy finding a new place to rent for her business and preparing to open, she would have no time for sleuthing. Of course, she'd emphatically agreed. "I'm leaving those days behind."

Her friends stared, unable to hide their shocked expressions.

"What?" Holly asked, growing defensive.

"You won't be able to help yourself." Charlene bit into a brownie.

Holly shrugged. "It's true. My sleuthing days are behind me. I'll be focusing on my business and my relationship with Trent."

"When's the wedding?" Charlene asked.

The blush rose in Holly's face. She felt it crawling up her neck. "We haven't set a date."

"No need to rush anything," Millicent said, then as if to cover, quickly added, "Though a fall wedding would be beautiful."

Holly smiled at her. She knew how hard it was, still, for Millicent, who'd had a crush on Trent for years. "Thank you. But we're focusing on our jobs at first." The thought of starting again was overwhelming, building loyal customers and working to be welcomed into the community. Holly knew from experience how much work lay ahead. Thankfully, the last she checked the local bakery had closed. If she moved fast, she could fill that spot.

"On that note." Millicent clapped. "Max?"

"Right away, Miss Millicent." Max reached behind the counter, his black shaggy hair trimmed so it wouldn't hide his eyes. He pulled out a huge gift basket and placed it at Holly's feet.

Last year, Holly had hired Max, a culinary student at the local high school. She was ecstatic that Millicent kept him on staff.

Millicent beamed. "It's from all of us. A going away gift basket. So you don't forget us peasant folk once you move to the city."

"It's not really a city. Just larger than Fairview." Holly tugged at the bow and pulled away the plastic wrapping.

"Woo wee." Charlene laughed. "Good thing Trent's not here."

The basket was filled with sleuthing stuff, a magnifying glass, an audio recorder, notebooks, pens. Of course, there were more non-mystery related items too: specialty baking tins, whisks, an apron, a coupon to Millicent's new shop.

"That's to make sure you come back to visit." Millicent winked.

"Thank you." Holly fought off the emotion. She dug deeper and pulled an item from the bottom. "What's this?"

Charlene studied it. "Never seen it before."

Millicent giggled. "You guys are so behind the times. It's a selfie stick. You know. You stick your phone on the end so you can more easily get group photos. That sort of thing."

Millicent lowered her voice. "You never know the clues you can capture with extended reach."

Holly laughed. "You seem convinced I'm going to dive headlong into a mystery."

"Of course you're not." Charlene couldn't hide the glimmer of mischief in her eyes. "It's just a way to remember all our escapades here. And take photos of you and Trent."

"Right."

***

Muffins curled in a ball on the seat next to her, snoring lightly. The air conditioning blasted and the music blared as Holly drove toward her new, but really old, stomping grounds. She'd grown up there and had moved to Fairview when her parents went into hiding. Thankfully, it had all been resolved, and Holly could return without a worry.

Time passed quickly, and soon, she drove the charming Main Street with quaint shops: a cozy antique store, used furniture, a wellness center, a gym, sporting goods. Everything and anything she could need or want. Even a restaurant with tables outside. She and Trent would have to check it out—soon! There were stoplights too, and more than a couple.

She rechecked the address she'd scribbled down. It was an apartment building in need of renters on the perimeter of town. After maneuvering the streets, Holly slowed to a crawl in front of the building.

Did she have the right one? She checked the address again. Yup. 32 Hickory Road. Holly studied the building, her mouth pursed. Hmm. Dandelions and weeds grew more thickly than grass. Paint peeled from the sides of the large house. Previously, it had been one dwelling, and a smart investor had broken it up into apartments. But now? It was in desperate need of a landscaper, or a landlord who cared. How hard was it whip out the lawnmower? This wasn't looking good. She'd hoped to sign the lease today. This one had sounded so good too. Also, there weren't any cars in the driveway. Did they have tenants?

Right then, a skinny older man, a flop of graying hair in his eyes, pushed a sad-looking mower around the corner. He didn't blink at the car parked at the curb. With long limbs and clothes that hung from his frame, he could use a few more cheesecakes in his life. She couldn't exactly drive away now. "What do you think, Muffins? Should we look?"

Muffins opened his eyes and yipped. Holly checked the time. Might as well. They were expecting her. Maybe the landlord was behind schedule. That was all. With Muffins tucked in her arms, Holly approached the man.

He yanked on the starter and the engine sputtered, then roared to life just as Holly approached.

"Excuse me!"

The man spit out of the corner of his mouth and muttered to himself. After a quick study, Holly determined he must be the landlord, as his clothes didn't appear dirty enough for someone who mowed and dug in the dirt most of the day.

"Excuse me! I have an appointment?" She shouted the last question.

He stopped, mower running, and looked her over. Disinterested, he shrugged her off and started mowing. Muffins growled.

The gall of this man. Holly couldn't help but stomp her foot. Didn't he want her business? Never mind. The more important question was—why was she still here?

"Time to leave, Muffins."

2

Holly had promised herself she wouldn't drop in to see Trent right away, but a part of her could use a little pick-me-up. The going-away party had left her nostalgic. And, no, she hadn't expected to find a place to live within the first ten minutes—but it would've been nice. As she remembered it, the station was bigger, more official and formal looking with its brick framework. Even she felt a bit intimidated.

"Let's go, Muffins. It's just Trent." After all, he was the new chief. She'd popped in often to say hello back in Fairview. "You be a good doggie here in my purse. Don't let anyone know you're with me." Somehow she didn't think they'd be impressed by a lady with a dog in her purse.

The inside of the office was just as formal as the outside. Holly shivered. It didn't scream friendly or we're-here-to-serve you. She approached the front desk. After a couple minutes, the cop finally, without looking up, said, "Can I help you?"

Holly swallowed and gathered her courage. What was wrong with her? There was no need to be nervous. "Yes, I'd like to see Trent Trinket, if he's available."

Long, awkward silence.

The man didn't seem to care too much about customer service. Even wearing the expected blue uniform, he didn't appear to hold any ranking of much importance. Holly would be bored with the job too.

"Name?" he said, after another couple minutes.

"Holly Hart."

"Second door on the right." He waved her past.

The second door on the right wasn't Trent's office. It was a small room with white walls. A metal table and two metal chairs were the only furniture. This wasn't an office. Maybe Trent took visitors in the interrogation room? She turned to ask someone, and the door shut.

"Hmm. That is interesting, Muffins."

She plunked down on the cold metal chair. Well, if she could say hi to Trent and make plans for later then sitting in this boring room would be worth it. She hadn't seen him in two weeks. Last weekend, he'd been too busy with a new case. Which reminded her, when she prodded for details, he was rather tight-lipped.

The doorknob turned.

Holly couldn't help it. She burst to her feet, a smile appearing before she could stop it. Not that she wanted to. She had so much to talk to him about. "Tr—"

It wasn't Trent.

A man with trimmed black hair and piercing green eyes entered—more like strode—confident and focused. A file was tucked under his arm, and when he placed it on the table, it was obvious the folder had seen some wear. The officer was young, probably under thirty, and had the potential to be handsome—if he'd smile. She pegged him right away as a young pup, anxious to prove himself and earn the respect of the force.

"Sit," he ordered, without introducing himself or even offering a smile to calm her nerves.

Sit? She wasn't a pet he could order around. "Excuse me. I'd like to see—"

"I'll ask the questions. You answer. It works well and goes smoothly if we both understand our roles in this. So, on the night in question—"

Holly giggled. She was waved through because they thought she was a witness! "Oh, no. I'm sorry. There must be—"

His gaze was sharp. "We're busy here. People call and come in with all sorts of claims that they hold break-through information on this big case. So far, it has been a waste of my time. Now, let's try this again. On the night—"

"Officer, Sir, really…" Holly had so many tidbits of wisdom to offer this young pup. First, his attitude and approach would more likely send a nervous witness running than encourage them to spill what they knew. He could use some lessons in charm and etiquette. And…wait. A gasp escaped. Was this connected to Trent's big case? The one he wasn't talking about because he'd decided their relationship shouldn't be based around her trying to solve his cases. No. As tempting as it was to milk this situation for information, she would be honest and explain this misunderstanding. "You see—"

"Ma'am." He sounded like a schoolteacher. Fire brimmed in his eyes. Holly felt sympathy as he'd probably interviewed hundreds. He was tired. He was annoyed. But she also felt shamed and humiliated. "There have three been murders. Three! We are working around the clock to prevent another one. Do you know something or not?"

Three murders! Trent had told her he'd been busy working, but he hadn't given specifics, like the tiny fact of three murders. Were they all connected? Holly's inquisitive mind flooded with questions. She felt she should've known about the murders, but she'd been so busy with the move she hadn't listened to the news.

She bit her lip, playing the role perfectly. "Three? Does that mean"—she lowered her voice to a whisper—"that we're looking at a…serial killer?" She clutched her purse while trying to read the scribbled upside-down notes on the page across from her.

He shifted the page closer and seemed to realize his mistake. His voice softened. "That is still being determined. No need to worry."

She caught sight of a word. "Were all the bodies found in a dumpster?" Her mind raced. That didn't necessarily mean this was a serial case. "I've watched all the episodes of Law & Order. I'm practically an expert, you know. Now"—she tapped her fingers on the table—"did the perp leave any kind of signature at the crime scene? You know, that's one clue that it is a serial case. If not, it could be…"

His eyes widened and jaw dropped slightly at her lecture.

"Wait"—she laughed—"What did you want to know?"

"Can you tell me anything about the night in question? Did you see anything suspicious?"

Holly squirmed. She wasn't about to give false information in hopes of learning more about the serial case. It wouldn't be right. "On what night?"

"You should know this." He sighed. "Friday night. Two weeks ago."

"What? A Friday? Oh my. I made a mistake. I thought it was Thursday. I was out of town on Friday." Which, technically, wasn't a lie.

"Wait a sec." He stood, hands splayed on the table, eyes narrowed. "Are you the witness who called earlier this morning?"

"Um, no." She stood, the desire to flee growing. "I guess I'll just be going. Sorry to waste your time."

She was at the door of the room, ready to run when he spoke. "I'm sorry, I didn't catch your name?"

She turned and flashed her own piercing gaze. "That's because I never said my name." She should stop. Bite her tongue. But she couldn't help it. "Just like you never stated yours. Good day, Officer. I wish you the best of luck." She opened the door and walked out.

Two seconds later, he shouted, "Harley!"

The cop behind the desk stood, his face pale.

Holly offered him a weak smile. He never should've waved her through without asking more questions. Poor guy. If she'd known why he chose to do that, she would've told him.

***

HOLLY COULDN'T WAIT for Trent. Armed with an ice-coffee, she reclined at one of the outside tables of the charming restaurant she learned was called, *Charlie's*. She half-focused on the newspaper she'd picked up hoping to find apartment rentals. As she skimmed the page, a prickle of guilt distracted her. Maybe Trent wouldn't hear about the red-haired woman who acted like a ditz and advised the interrogating officer on concepts of serial killers, never mind wasting his time. She also wished she could read upside-down better. She chuckled to herself. Maybe she should carry the selfie stick in her purse. She could've asked for a selfie with Officer Ice and captured his notes in the background.

She flipped through the paper, hoping to find something on the murders. Toward the back, she found it. The title read: Can the new chief prove his worth?

Her gaze skimming, she caught the barest of details, most of which she knew from her conversation at the station. Three murders. All the bodies found in dumpsters. The focus of the article was Trent, and the lack of forward motion on the case. No wonder she hadn't heard from him. He had to be working night and day to prove himself as the new chief.

The next few minutes she spent scouring the internet for previous articles. The town paper blocked full access; it required a subscription. She definitely wasn't in Kansas any more.

Finally, the ice melted in her glass, she realized that sitting there would get her nowhere. Maybe a trip to the library was in order. They had to have copies of the local papers—without charging! She could escape the heat and find a quiet corner somewhere.

She scanned the rest of the page with no success. Eventually, she noticed a line winding down the sidewalk. She scratched the top of Muffins' head as he wiggled in her purse. "Let's go see what's causing all the commotion."

Main Street was quaint, perfect for business if she could find a place to rent. The large town had made effort with benches and lampposts, freshly painted lines, and potted flowers. The winding line was growing. What kind of business would create such a customer base willing to wait that long? Every business owner dreamed of long lines. She walked faster, squinting, trying to catch a peek at the sign above the heads of the people.

Her heart sank. What? When did this happen? Impossible. But no, it wasn't impossible. It was staring her in the face.

She wished she hadn't noticed the crowd. Just seeing the sign made her want to become a patron. It was amazing how smart branding and design could affect a potential customer. In colors of green and orange, which she never would've paired, but somehow worked, the sign protruded from the top of the door.

The Pie Crust.

A bakery.

Had it popped up over night? Just opened this morning? That would explain the interest on the first day. She hoped to find space on Main Street. Not that competition wasn't good and healthy. It was. So why did she feel such dismay? She'd left Fairview brimming with hope and excitement, the future bright. Well, she would've been brimming with excitement once she got over the emotional goodbyes. Now? Holly brimmed with disappointment.

"Excuse me, miss. Are you in line?" a man asked.

"What?" She glanced at the sign again. "No, no. Go ahead." She couldn't muster the enthusiasm to enter. Not yet. Instead, she crossed the street and plunked down on a bench and stared at the competition, brooding.

The stewing only increased as she studied the waiting patrons of *The Pie Crust*. Business men and women, moms with strollers, singles, couples: every kind of customer. Happy, smiling faces streamed out of the bakery, hands full of pastries.

Except for one.

A man exited, clearly unhappy. Muttering and grumbling. The breadth of his waist suggested he was a daily patron of *The Pie Crust*. Holly hated that she felt the glimmer of satisfaction at his discontent with her future competition. She would never actually wish for a company to do poorly. What was their secret?

The man strutted across the street and then, much to Holly's delight, sat next to her on the bench.

Seemed a wasted opportunity to say nothing.

"*The Pie Crust* out of your favorite pastry?" she asked with a smile. "Frosting a little too sweet?"

He hesitated, before acting like he would even answer her attempt at conversation. His thinning gray hair swooped across his forehead, and his nose appeared to have been broken at some point. He had the air and posture of a man who acted above his station. Untouchable.

She didn't honestly expect him to answer.

"Oh no, nothing like that. I was threatened."

3

THE PAPERS WITH HER references in hand, Holly firmly knocked on the door. She took several deep breaths, eyes closed, to calm her expression. No need to appear desperate.

Surprise and delight could only have explained Holly's reaction when she'd noticed the sign behind the bench. What luck! It said Apartment for Rent. Perfect. After a morning that hadn't gone as hoped or planned, this could be the turning point. Never mind processing what the man had said outside. Threatened? She hadn't been able to poke further, because he'd stormed away, still furious.

When the door opened, Holly plastered on a bright smile that she hoped said, 'I'll make the perfect tenant.'

"Hello there." The woman who opened the door was older, middle-aged, and by the worn expression, messy ponytail, stained shirt, and the cry from the background, most likely, a mom.

"Yes, I'm interested in the apartment for rent." She handed over the papers. "Here are my references."

"Sure." She accepted the papers and took a few minutes to read them over. Then, she reached back and grabbed a key. "Marcy, I'll be right back. Keep an eye on Jack." She shut the door. "Follow me. It's right up the stairs."

"Do you own the building?" Holly studied the clean walls and shiny light fixtures as they walked.

"No. I'm a renter. They offered to knock down my rent if I was available to show apartments." At the door, she stopped. "Where are my manners? I'm Shelly." She stuck out a hand to shake. "Is it just you?"

"I'm Holly." She smiled. "Just me and Muffins." She opened her purse. "Are pets allowed?"

"Yes." Shelly opened the door to a bright apartment.

Holly walked through, delighted. She and Trent had talked about it and both of them wanted to wait until after they were married to move in together. The apartment was nothing fancy, but it was clean and spacious. A small kitchen/living room open concept, and a hallway led to the bedroom and bathroom. What drew her attention immediately was the large window that looked over Main Street. "Ooh, I love it!"

"Yes, it's the only one with a view. There are three apartments. I'm downstairs, and an elderly gentleman is right across the hall from you. He's a bit grumpy, but harmless. Rent is expected the first of the month. A one-year lease. One thousand a month."

She might find something cheaper if she had the time to look but this seemed perfect, and she needed somewhere to crash. Yes, she could always spend the night on Trent's couch, but she was anxious to get started looking at real estate for *Just Cheesecake*. Even though she was ready to sign on the dotted line, Holly paused, then asked, "Just curious, Shelly, but do you know anything about these dumpster murders I've heard about?"

"Oh yes, it's horrible." Shelly grimaced. "I don't know much. Just what I've read. So far there have been three, all men. They don't seem to be connected, from what I can tell."

Holly entered the familiar territory of analyzing a murder. "It seems more than coincidence that all the bodies were left in dumpsters though."

"True." Shelly shrugged.

"Did the papers say there was anything unique about the murders? Anything to connect them?"

"Um…" Shelly placed a hand on her hip. "I think there was poison involved? Or maybe they had all been stabbed? I don't know."

"Had they been near here at all?"

"No. Thank God." Shelly walked toward the window, and Holly followed. "But lucky us, we have *The Pie Crust* right across the street to chase away the nightmares."

Once more, Holly stared out the window at the line that seemed to have grown even longer. "Yes, I haven't been in yet. Is it always this popular?" Holly asked, casually.

"Oh yes. I thought it might die down after the opening week. But it has been a month and it remains popular."

"The pastries must be mouth watering for customers to be willing to wait in that line."

"Yes, well, it is the only place to go, and for more than just the pastries."

"Why is that?" Holly asked.

Shelly laughed. "Oh, you'll see. I don't want to ruin first impressions." She turned away from the window. "So, interested in the place?"

Holly looked around once more. "Yes, I think I am."

"I'll be right back with the papers and you can move in today."

After the rental agreement had been signed and Shelly left for the second time, Holly let Muffins out of her purse. "There you go. Freedom."

Muffins yipped and raced around the room. Holly found herself back at the window, staring at *The Pie Crust*. First impressions—what had Shelly meant by that? Clearly, the owner offered some kind of secondary attraction. It didn't take long to brush off those thoughts. Eventually, she'd have to visit the shop to find out. Just not today.

Leaning against the window seat, she studied the room. It wouldn't need much. She already had a sofa, armchair, and coffee table. The movers would eventually bring everything, including her kitchen equipment and other boxes. What she was most excited about was christening her new kitchen with some cheesecakes. But first, she'd need to unpack.

"You stay here, Muffins. I'll be back." After locking up, she hurried down the street to her car, ignoring the line of customers at *The Pie Crust*. If she was fast, there was a spot right in front of her apartment building.

Minutes later, she was parked and unloading the car. Boxes packed with cookbooks and cooking utensils came first. If she made a quick trip to the grocery store, she could start baking tonight. A strawberry cheesecake with a glass of wine would be the perfect way to end the day. Maybe a visit with Trent. Heck, she'd be happy with a phone conversation.

On her fourth trip, Holly realized she'd underestimated the heat and the stairs. She plunked down a box outside her door and sat on it. Muffins barked from inside. "Okay, okay." She opened the door to let him out. He raced back and forth in the hall, yipping up a storm. "Sorry, I don't have a ball."

With a sigh, she continued. On her fifth trip, she arrived at the top of the stairs to find an elderly gentleman standing in the hall. He stood slightly hunched over, leaning on a cane. She was about to offer a cheerful welcome when she noticed his sour expression. His mouth was puckered, like he'd sucked on a lemon. And his eyebrows were lowered over sharp eyes. He might be old but she could see intelligence. She would definitely have to bake him a cheesecake.

"Hi, I'm Holly." She stuck out her hand, which he ignored.

"Trouble maker. That's what you are," he grumped.

"Excuse me. I am no such thing." She was curious, sometimes too curious, but she was not a troublemaker in the way he suggested.

He pointed his cane at her. "What's causing all that racket, then? Bumping and thumping." He narrowed his eyes. "Do you have a gorilla in there or something? Just when I thought I'd have some peace and quiet, someone moves in. Just my luck. I was hoping for at least a month of rest. Do you play loud rock music too? Throw big parties? Well, don't even think about it. I'll call the police so fast your head will spin. I have connections, you know. And I'm not afraid to use them."

She spoke in a calm, friendly tone. "I'm moving in. I don't normally make a lot of noise, but my dog, Muffins, has been cooped up in my purse all day, and he's excited." She decided to be sassy back. "I hope you don't play reruns of Jeopardy too loud in the evening. If so, I'll have to complain."

"Aha! Trouble maker, I knew it." Muffins barked.

"And a dog named Muffins? What did he do to deserve that?"

"Muffins is a perfectly good name. I'm a baker and it seemed to fit."

"You're a baker, huh?"

"Yes."

"Have a place of business yet?"

"Not yet. I just moved in today."

"Well, good luck." He hesitated, glancing at the stairs and then back at Holly. "Where's your boyfriend or brother to help you lug your stuff up the stairs?"

"I am quite capable." Except she had to admit she would've enjoyed the help.

"Leave the rest. My godson is visiting tonight." He stopped, thinking, then scratched his head. "Well, he often doesn't make it because of work, but he'll be here in the next couple of days. He'll carry the rest up. Unless you're one of those stubborn females who insist on doing everything yourself."

Holly wanted to make a crack back, but she had no desire to make a contentious neighbor even grumpier. "I'd like that. Thank you."

"You're welcome." He shuffled back inside his apartment. "And you'd better be right about little cupcake there."

"That's Muffins to you, thank you very much." But the friendly neighbor had already slammed his door.

4

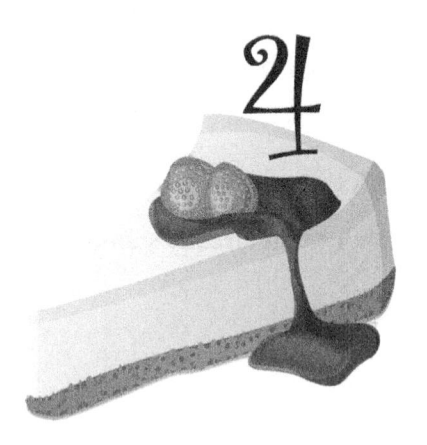

Holly had been in town for almost twenty-four hours and still no word from Trent. She'd been in an empty apartment, waiting for the movers to arrive. It wasn't much. And she was bored, left alone, stewing about *The Pie Crust* and the serial murder case she didn't really know much about.

Certainly, if Officer Ice with the arresting green eyes had mentioned her to Trent, if he had described her, then Trent, even if exhausted, would've stopped by to scold her properly. She giggled. He would at least try. Then a brilliant idea appeared in her mind. Why hadn't she thought of this before? If he was too busy or too tired to come to her, she would go to him. Make a nice dinner, have drinks ready. He had to eat. Right?

Muffins had declared his favorite napping spot and that was by the window. The same window that looked out over her competition. She'd been trying not to count the people in line at various times of the day. But she also loved gazing at Main Street. The early morning light glinted off benches and lampposts, and joggers and dog walkers were out in full force. Later, businessmen and women would hunt for a bite to eat to get them through to the end of the day, and then, by mid-afternoon, the moms and dads with strollers and young children would hit the streets. Okay, so maybe she hadn't stayed away from the window as much as she thought.

She left Muffins napping, already having taken him on several walks the day before. Then, dressed in a casual pastel blue sundress, perfect for this heat, and for seeing her fiancé, she left for the grocery store. Two hours until dinner. That left enough time to shop and whip up a delicious meal at Trent's.

The grocery store was packed as it was nearing dinner but she managed to pick up veggies and steak tips in record time. Certainly, his grill was up and working.

As she waited in line, two full carts long, she did what she loved: observe people. Even though she'd only been gone a little over a year, she realized that previously living in her parents' home in a gated community had kept her from meeting the people in town. Most of her high school friends had moved. It was almost like she was living in a new place. That might not be a bad thing. Of course, if she stopped by at the country club, she'd know all her parents' friends.

After standing in line about ten minutes, her gaze focused on the man in front of her. Thinning gray hair, and a rather hefty, proud stature. How had she not recognized him earlier? She was about to jest about his threat the day before, see if he'd recovered, and maybe learn more about it, when his phone rang. A standard ring. Nothing trendy like a bird chirping or a famous rock song.

She grabbed a magazine she didn't intend to read or buy, and held it in front of her face. Nothing too obvious.

"I will be there at the expected time…no, you don't understand." He huffed and his shift in stance revealed his extreme annoyance while the person on the other end prattled on. "No, I will not give you more time or be more flexible. I have already been more than generous. I will do my job. What ever happens is not my fault, but most likely, your own incompetence in keeping up with your responsibilities…" He let out an audible, shocked gasp. "I do not appreciate that. Good day."

Holly peeked over the magazine. A mottled red crept up the back of the man's neck. He was clearly peeved. It was his turn in line, and Holly watched as he placed his food in a particular order on the belt, ordering and re-ordering the items. Again, muttering to himself.

"Find everything you need?" the young and pretty cashier asked.

"Yes, yes." He answered like he didn't really hear her, and then kept muttering.

Holly decided it was time to speak up. "Another bad day, huh?"

He gave her a cursory glance, didn't respond or seem to recognize her, and then carried his bags out of the store, strutting like he was on a mission.

Holly shrugged it off, purchased her groceries, and then headed to Trent's. Bags in hand, she found the key in the potted plant and entered. It was her turn to gasp.

The place was a disaster.

Pizza boxes and frozen food wrappers littered the coffee table and kitchen counter. A laundry basket filled with clothes, which she didn't know if they were dirty or clean, sat by the couch. She felt bad for wishing he'd had more time for her. He usually wasn't this messy. She hadn't realized until today and reading the paper how big this serial case had become. Of course, it was. He wanted to make a good impression.

Time to work and help him out. While the steak tips and veggies marinated in foil packets, Holly attacked the mess. Just clearing the room of trash made the place so much cleaner. It wasn't until she poked around at the papers and trash on the coffee table that she slowed. Some of the papers were scribbled with notes.

Of course, she wouldn't look at them.

She shifted them while picking up the trash. She vacuumed and dumped clothes into the washing machine. She wiped down counters and washed dishes. And she didn't mind one bit because she knew it was helping Trent.

Finally, with a glass of water, and wondering when Trent would be home as it was nearing seven o'clock, she flopped on the couch. The case notes were tantalizing, sitting there, begging to be read. She shook her head. Nope. She wouldn't. Arms folded, she refused to give in.

Minutes passed.

Trent still wasn't home.

Must be a long day, as in he might not be home until late. How many nights did he put in these extra hours? It couldn't be healthy. She didn't want to admit that she might be sitting there for a while when she could be home unpacking or baking. Maybe her neighbor's godson had stopped by, waiting for her. She could use the help. Of course, the grumpy old man might not have followed through either.

With a sigh, she admitted that her evening wouldn't be the romantic reunion she'd envisioned. She jotted a note and left it on the counter.

At the door, hand on the knob, she hesitated. One peek wouldn't hurt. It wasn't like he'd locked the notes away in a desk. They were on the coffee table for anyone to see.

After peering out the window, she approached the coffee table, her footsteps silent on the carpet. Dusting! That was it. The table could definitely use a good dusting. Finding a cloth under the sink, she wiped the table, moving papers as needed. It wasn't exactly snooping if she happened to see something. No one dusted with their eyes closed.

Two minutes later, because dusting doesn't take that long, she locked the door behind her and headed home.

***

HOLLY HESITATED IN the hall of her apartment building. Should she ask if the man's godson had stopped by? She needed to at least learn her neighbor's name. They were neighbors, after all. Feeling the exhaustion of the day, Holly decided to leave it and entered her apartment. Muffins greeted her, yipping and running circles.

"Yes, yes." She sighed. "We'll go for a walk in a minute."

Thankfully, she'd brought the basic necessities for baking. She eyed the mixer and knew the fridge was packed with ingredients to make the first cheesecake in her new home, but it would have to wait until the next day. Sleep was calling.

"Fetch your leash."

While Muffins obeyed, she flattened empty boxes. She hadn't asked about recycling or about the schedule of the trash truck. Boxes tucked under her arm, she led Muffins outside.

The heat wave hadn't stopped so late evening had to be appreciated with the slightly cooler air. This humidity meant a thunderstorm would eventually hit. Enjoying the evening, Holly let Muffins lead. "Find me a trash can or dumpster, Muffins."

As they walked, Holly went back to brooding on just about everything. She wasn't sure living across the street from *The Pie Crust* was a smart choice. Waking up to the reminder of the bakery's success might not be good for her morale. It was probably the exhaustion but at that moment she felt like opening day for her pastry shop was weeks away. First, she had to find a place to rent. And Trent? Hopefully she would see him soon. The quick texts here and there weren't enough. Thoughts struck like lightning bolts. First about Trent and the notes she'd read, and then the next second, she'd think about *The Pie Crust*. Eventually, she'd have to stop and sample the goods.

Before Holly knew it, Muffins had led her down a side alley a couple of blocks from her apartment. Nearby businesses used it but tossing in cardboard boxes seemed harmless.

Muffins bounded down the alley, tugging hard on the leash.

"I'm coming. I'm coming."

She arrived in front of the dumpster out of breath. Muffins barked up a storm. The thought appeared all at once. Muffins barking in front of the dumpster, the notes on Trent's coffee table, the time of night. It all seemed rather ominous. She should just walk away. But what if…

Using a wooden box that sat off to the side, Holly stepped on it and peeked into the dumpster. "Ugh." The smell of rotten food and trash made her gag. She used the flashlight on her phone, and at first, didn't see anything unusual.

Wait a second. She looked closer.

Was that an arm?

5

Yes, it was definitely an arm.

Right next to the hunk of rotten lettuce and carrots, and overloaded, leaking trash bags. Muffins' barking faded, everything faded. She'd seen enough crime scenes to not be shocked or grossed out by a dead body. Instead, her analytical mind took over.

She narrowed in on the arm and then scanned the rest of the garbage. What appeared to be a stomach bulged from underneath restaurant take-home boxes. And, at the far end, a man's black dress shoe poked through the sludge. He looked to be about five foot eleven, almost six feet.

This was definitely a crime. An apparently well-dressed man wouldn't be snoozing in the trash like this. Nor would he be digging for leftovers with a well-defined, protruding waistline.

She climbed down, realizing she shouldn't have moved the wooden box. She placed it back where she found it and then studied the ground surrounding the dumpster. There wasn't much. No obvious footprints or telltale clues—like a murder weapon. That would be too easy.

Discovering a body was one way to catch Trent's attention. She jabbed in his personal number and waited until she was sent to voicemail. "Hi Trent. Give me a call back asap. I found something you might be interested in, as a cop."

Should she call the station and report the crime—or wait for Trent to call?

"Put your hands where I can see them!" A sharp and commanding voice echoed down the alley. It didn't sound like Trent. "This is the police."

Muffins barked. "Sit," Holly hissed. Thankfully, he obeyed. "They're up. They're up. I-I was just throwing away some of my boxes. Is there a problem, Officer?" She hated that she sounded nervous, stuttering like a newbie when it came to a crime scene. She'd been at plenty. Probably more than a beat cop. Wait. Did this officer know about the body? Or was he making rounds?

"What are you doing?"

Honesty was usually the best policy. "I was walking my dog and decided to throw away some boxes. You see, I just moved into the area. Yesterday, in fact. I used the wooden box that's to my left and tossed the boxes into the dumpster. That's when I noticed—"

"I don't need your life story, yet." He stepped closer. A blinding light flashed in her eyes. After pacing around the dumpster and completing a short study of the area, he used the same box to peer into the dumpster.

"I know exactly what you'll find." Holly still couldn't get a good look at the cop. Her phone buzzed but she couldn't answer.

He hesitated.

"Can I answer my phone? I'm expecting a personal call." She wanted to throw in the fact that it was probably Chief Trinket but decided against it.

"No." He shined his light into the dumpster.

"To the right you'll find a pale arm next to the day-old lettuce. Down and to the left you'll see the protruding belly of a wealthy man. And near the left corner, a once-shiny fancy men's shoe can be seen. I've deduced that he's upper class and about five foot eleven."

The officer didn't respond at first, which left Holly time to think. He seemed to know about the body. Why else would he be here? This was a relatively safe neighborhood. "I assume you received a call about the body."

"Yes." Slowly, he climbed down and turned. The glare off her face, Holly recognized him at once and inwardly groaned. Officer Ice. The same one she'd not been completely honest with the day before. He recognized her simultaneously and his eyes narrowed. She decided to play up the Law & Order enthusiast again.

"I called the station right away. I can't believe the service. You appeared fast. I looked for a weapon but didn't see any. Of course, I knew better than to climb into the dumpster and search for one. I knew to leave that to the forensics team."

"Really," he said, drily. "How savvy of you."

Ooh, he was so cocky. The look of disdain and disbelief rubbed her the wrong way. She continued, "Is it normal for the murderer to call in and report the crime? That seems rather odd."

"Who said it was the murderer?" he asked.

"Who else would it be?" She glanced around. "I don't see anyone waiting. And dead bodies always draw attention. You know, morbid fascination. It must be the murderer." Maybe that was the signature. Might as well poke the bear. "Is this part of the serial murders you were asking me about yesterday? Maybe the call-in is the signature because I certainly didn't see anything strange in the dumpster. Were there call-ins with the previous murders?" She already knew the answer from peeking at Trent's notes. There had been no call-ins with any of them.

"There are many different ways a killer can leave a signature. And the details of the case are none of your business."

Her temper flared. "I was just trying to help, Officer…? I'm sorry I didn't catch your name."

He ignored her obvious question and placed the call to the station asking for the forensics team. "Yup, add another one to the list."

She glared at him, shocked. He assumed that this body was connected to the others. Why wouldn't he talk to Trent directly and let him know this couldn't be connected?

With the previous murders, citizens discovered the bodies.

No clues left behind at the crime scene.

No DNA. Not even a hair.

The serial killer was meticulous, as most were. That had to be his or her signature—that there was no signature. No, this murder could very well be a copycat, or someone hoping that blame would be placed on the serial killer. But, of course, this latest copycat murderer hadn't cleaned Trent's apartment and happened upon the case notes to know the details.

She couldn't help but add in her two cents, get this officer thinking. "You know, this could very well be a copycat or someone hoping to get away with murder, thinking the police will assume it's the serial killer." She left it at that and then studied him, hoping to learn something from his reaction.

But he was good. His face remained expressionless with the usual annoyance. Was it just her, or was he like this all the time?

Then he turned on her. "Maybe you're the killer." He didn't pace or flinch. "Maybe you stopped by yesterday pretending to be a witness. Or, you just couldn't help but flaunt yourself in front of the police. A sick and twisted killer. And then tonight, with your…morbid fascination, you called the police, impatient, and then waited for us to show so you could play the role of ally. Or maybe, desperate for recognition, you were afraid this latest victim wouldn't be found." He pulled out his cuffs and stepped closer. Muffins growled.

Holly cleared her throat and mustered up some courage. "Do you always go around accusing innocent citizens of being sick and twisted?" She turned her focus away from his behavior. "Sorry that doesn't make sense at all. I'm much too smart. If I were to kill someone…" She stopped. That didn't sound good.

He raised an eyebrow. "Please don't stop. What would you do if you were to kill someone?" He crossed his arms, cuffs dangling from his fingers. "I'd love to know."

Sirens sounded in the distance. Holly's throat went dry. If Trent were to show, this wouldn't look good. She hadn't even been here two days before getting caught up in a murder. She talked fast. "Well, first, I would never be a serial killer. I'm not that sick."

"But you might be smart enough to jump onto a serial murder to get away with murder." He nodded. "As you suggested earlier."

"Yes, but I wouldn't then report the body and wait for a cop to show at the scene. Nor"—her voice raised a notch—"would I then suggest to the cop my methods." She huffed. "I mean, really. I'd leave the country, at least the state."

"Thanks. I'll keep all that in the file I'll start on you when I get back to the station. Miss…?"

She snorted. "Like I would tell you my name after all your insults." This probably wasn't the right time to ask. "Can I lower my arms? They're tired. You see, I've been unpacking and lifting boxes…"

The piercing glare he sent her way was a clear no.

The sirens grew close. A door closed. Footsteps sounded. "Detective Howe, is there a problem?"

It was Trent.

6

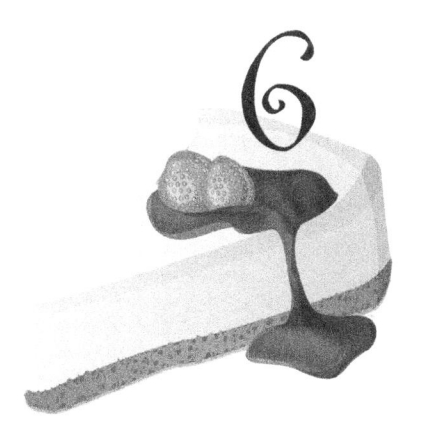

HOLLY TRIED HER BEST to press into the shadows. It wasn't easy. Muffins recognized Trent and let out a yip. It was very possible Trent would be so involved in the crime scene that she could slink away. Surely, Detective Howe—it was nice to know his name—wouldn't want to show his ineptitude to his boss. Accusing a citizen of being a serial killer. Overall rudeness.

This wasn't how she'd envisioned her reunion with Trent. In fact, it was quite the opposite.

He walked out of the shadows, his stride confident. Her heart squeezed. She wanted to run and leap into his arms and kiss him passionately, but this was definitely not the time or place. Seeing him in uniform was pure eye candy. His sandy hair was combed perfectly. But there was more if one looked closely. He was tired. She could see it in his eyes and the way he stood tall to compensate for the exhaustion.

"Where's the body?" Trent asked, his gaze sweeping the area and the dark corners of the alley. He wasn't one to be caught off guard.

Of course, he was too skilled as a cop to not be aware of his surroundings. Holly pressed against the brick building, hands still up. But if he noticed her, he didn't acknowledge it. Was that a hint of a smirk on his face—or fury?

Detective Howe lost his cocky attitude and became the professional. "Yes, Sir. Victim is a white male, seems to be upper class, about five and eleven inches by my estimation."

Holly stifled a gasp. That worm! He used her exact words.

"Excellent." Trent nodded.

"Chief, there's a concern I need to bring to your attention—"

"Hold on, Howe."

The forensics team swarmed the alley with kits and tools, ready to extract the body and then pick through the trash. Holly didn't envy them that stinky job, but she was thankful they arrived right when Howe was about to expose her to Trent. Howe called her a concern. Geez. She found the body, and he was treating her like a suspect, just because he could, because she'd annoyed him.

The team worked to pull out the body and laid it on a rolling cart to be delivered to the morgue. At first glance, Holly didn't see any obvious injuries. No wounds to the body or head trauma. No bruises or marks around the neck. His clothing didn't appear to be torn, just the normal wear and tear of having been transported, probably in the trunk of a car, and then thrown into a dumpster. Of course, the light wasn't the best in an alley. Most likely, his death had been a surprise. Either an attack from behind, suffocation, or possibly poison. That was her best guess.

"Okay, cover him up. I want a full report as soon as possible." Trent addressed the forensic team. "I want anything that looks suspicious. Anything that could've been a weapon. Or possible personal items, notes or receipts, which might've fallen from this man's pocket. I want a complete study and write up on my desk yesterday," he barked.

She should sneak away while Howe was distracted, but she'd never get this chance again. Once more, Holly studied the corpse. Her gaze landed on his face and thinning gray hair. She flashed back to the scene at the bench and the flustered phone call in the grocery store. She had to bite her lip from shouting out that she recognized him. Not his name or occupation. But there was much she could tell the cops about this man from bumping into him in the past couple days. That meant she couldn't stay in the shadows.

"Excuse me." She stepped forward. Did she still need her hands in the air? She lowered them.

Trent stiffened. Maybe he hadn't seen her. It wasn't like she could've escaped this scene without drawing attention to herself. Might as well make a splash.

"Not now, Miss." Detective Howe spoke in a condescending manner. "But I'll take your name and number. We'll want an official statement in the morning."

She stepped closer and Trent faced her. They caught eyes and his message to her was clear: *How in the world did you get involved in this? And you'd better have a good explanation. And, this is the end of your interest in this case.*

Of course, now he would tell her even less about it. He didn't acknowledge right away that he knew her, probably just as caught off guard with this unromantic reunion as she felt.

After a nod of recognition on her part, she said, "I know this man."

That got their attention. Trent's eyebrows shot into his hairline. Detective Howe was a bit less surprised. "Shocking. Please share your expert opinion. But remember anything you say can be held against you."

She refused to be cowered or intimidated by this cocky cop. "I first saw this man the other day when he left *The Pie Crust*." She thought back on the incident. "He was quite flustered, more like angry and insulted. I was sitting on the bench across the street, and to my surprise, he came straight for me, muttering the whole time. Then he sat next to me."

Detective Howe huffed. "Remember, this isn't an episode of Law and Order."

Trent remained quiet but thoughtful.

"It was obvious to me at the time that this man was not only upper class but full of himself. Quite arrogant."

"And pray tell how did you know that?" Howe shot out.

"He had an air about him. I wouldn't be surprised if daily interactions with people caused him angst. Anyway, he was definitely upset. I used a bit of humor and asked if the frosting was too sweet or if the bakery was out of his favorite dessert." She paused, then said, "He told me he'd been threatened. And then he walked away before I could ask anything else."

"Thank you very much. If you remember anything else—"

"Oh, that's not all."

Trent folded his arms and assumed a casual stance. "You interacted with the victim twice?"

"Yes. I can tell you that this man is very particular. He's not one for frills or extravagances. He's no nonsense. And when upset or when things don't go as planned, he tends to get upset, sometimes rightly so, and other times not. He likes things in order and in their place. A bit of an obsessive-compulsive disorder."

Trent gaped, which sent thrills running through Holly. He was impressed. Ever since her experiences in Fairview, she'd been working on her observation skills and interpreting behaviors. It was a game she played. More for the fun of it, not because she'd hoped to be involved in a murder case any time soon.

Howe was ruffled not impressed. "And, can you tell us his girlfriend's name and whether he likes ketchup or mustard on his hotdogs?"

"In fact, I can. He most definitely would use neither ketchup nor mustard. He cares about his appearance so would never take the risk of a blob of mustard or drip of ketchup staining his clothes. I'd go so far as to say he doesn't eat hotdogs but snacks on caviar and shrimp in the privacy of his home."

The tension in the air spiked, and Detective Howe shifted his stance.

Holly wasn't done. "Earlier this afternoon, I was in the grocery store picking up ingredients to make dinner for my fiancé. You see, he's been extremely busy, and since moving to town I hadn't seen him yet." Holly didn't feel satisfied when Trent blushed. But he did seem to soften a bit, which had been the intended effect. "The most important part of standing behind the man in the grocery store was a phone call he received. I don't remember everything, because at the time I didn't know it would be important or that he was soon to be murdered."

"You didn't take notes?" Howe asked.

"That's enough, Howe." Trent faced Holly and asked more gently. "What do you remember of the conversation?"

Holly thought back but couldn't remember the exact words. But the tone had been clear. "The person on the other end was upset, and this man"—she pointed to the body—"didn't respond well. He mentioned something about a job, so it was probably business related, rather than personal."

"Anything else?" Trent asked.

"No, that's it."

"Thank you very much. You've been a big help. If you could stop by the station tomorrow for an official statement, that would be great. Until then, see if you can remember any more of the phone call." With a quick nod, he dismissed her.

Howe scowled. "Chief, maybe we should bring her down now for questioning. She was in the alley when I arrived and seemed to know a bit too much about the serial case."

Terrific, Holly thought. Now Trent would guess she'd read his notes or had been fishing for information. She'd have to answer to him later. He wasn't about to reveal that he was her boyfriend, that they were engaged. Not now. Did she embarrass him?

"I don't think that's necessary, Detective Howe." Trent studied the forensics team working. "We're done here. I'll see you at the office bright and early, and hopefully, we'll have some clues to study."

After receiving a scathing look from Detective Howe, Holly decided that was her cue to leave. She gathered Muffins in her arms, and left.

***

It was midnight.

Holly paced in her living room, peering out the window every few minutes. The coffee gurgled. The strong aroma filled the studio apartment. A plate of chocolate chip cookies sat on the table. She'd whipped them up as soon as she returned home. Yes, it was late, but she expected Trent any second. He might've gone straight home, but most likely, he'd returned to the office, then home. He'd see her note with the new address at the bottom, eat his dinner while debating between sleep and visiting her, and then drive over, if only for a proper reunion—and scolding.

There was no way she could sit still because she had no idea how he would process seeing her at the crime scene. It wasn't her fault that she'd had two interactions with the victim. Had Trent come to the conclusion that this most recent murder wasn't connected to the serial case? Or maybe there was more she didn't know about those murders. She sighed. It wasn't like he would tell her.

She should stop thinking about it right now, forget everything, but her heart pounded and her mind raced. She couldn't help it. After all, she needed to attempt to recall the phone conversation. Thinking about the case and writing down what she knew so far might help.

Millicent's gift of a notebook and pen would be used earlier than expected. With a cup of steaming coffee, and notebook on her lap, Holly sat on the floor and leaned against the wall. She tapped the pencil on the paper. First, there were the serial murders. This latest one didn't seem connected to the others, but it was still a possibility. She swore by her description of the man, his airs. She remembered the way he kept moving groceries on the belt, like he was never quite happy with how they were positioned. Or maybe he was nervous, fidgeting from the anxiety caused by the phone call. Something to do with work.

She tried to make a list of words hoping one would jar her memory. Jobs, work, responsibility, follow-through, unhappy clients. Nothing triggered any sort of recall.

A light knock on the door. "Holly? You awake?"

Quickly, Holly closed the notebook and shoved it in a kitchen drawer. "Coming!" She rushed to open the door. "Hi!" She sounded breathless, nervous.

"Hi, there." There it was. The same endearing smile she'd missed for two weeks. "Do you have time?"

"Of course." Did he have to ask? "Want a cup?"

"Would love one."

"Sorry I have no place to sit. I just found the apartment yesterday, and the movers aren't coming until tomorrow with my furniture. Of course, I had to at least bring my baking supplies with me. This wouldn't properly be home until I'd used the kitchen." She replenished her cup, and then joined Trent against the wall.

"Thank you." He wrapped his hand around the warmth. "Exactly what I needed." Then he added softly, "Thank you for the dinner." He fell silent. Apparently, the way the coffee swirled in his cup was fascinating.

"Are you mad?" Holly whispered.

7

Trent didn't say anything at first, and then sighed. "No, I'm not mad."

"Disappointed?"

He turned a tired but honest gaze on her. "I'm trying to piece together how you knew all that about the victim. How you managed to get on the bad side of my top detective so fast."

"He's a pompous—"

"Yes, but he's good. The best around. His instinct is close to perfect. What he lacks in charm he makes up for in skill."

"To say he lacks charm is to put it nicely." Holly desperately wanted to tell him how Detective Howe insulted her at the station and at the crime scene, but that would only cause problems at work. That was the last thing she wanted.

"We believe we found the man's wallet," Trent said.

Whoa. Information. That was the last thing Holly expected. "What's his name?"

"I'll find out in the morning."

Trent was usually honest with her, but she couldn't help but wonder if that was a fib. "You can tell me his name. What do you think I'm going to do—break into his house or something and hunt for clues?"

"Well…"

Okay, it was definitely a fib. Trent knew the man's name. "I didn't go looking for this. I couldn't help that I bumped into the man before he was murdered."

"I believe you…" His hesitation spoke volumes. "But my detective isn't convinced. He said you lied the other day at the station."

Oh, brother. She'd forgotten about that. "True. I stopped by to say a quick hello. They didn't ask and I didn't tell and the next thing I knew they waved me into the interrogation room. Detective Howe came in and threw questions at me. Never gave me a chance to explain why I was there." She shrugged. "I played along. It might've helped if you'd told me how big and important this case was." She winced. This wasn't his fault, and she hated implying that. "I'm just saying it would've helped if I'd known the bare essentials."

He drained the coffee. "Fine. You might as well tell me what you know."

"About what?" Holly blinked innocently.

"The big case."

"I don't know that much." Holly wasn't sure she should admit what she knew because some of it came by underhanded means, like reading words upside-down.

Trent flashed her a look that said, yeah, right. "I'd rather you just tell me."

Fine. But he asked for it. "Let's see. There have been three murders. Most likely connected. A serial murderer. The bodies are always left in a dumpster, but the murder never happens there. The killer is meticulous in that he leaves nothing behind. No DNA or anything. And, he uses poison." That was her best guess anyway given the lack of obvious injury to the body she found. "But, this most recent one probably isn't connected because the murderer called it in. That's never happened. It's someone trying to get away with murder."

Trent raked a hand through his hair. "How did you know there were three?"

"Detective Howe told me." Then she added softly, "It's also in the papers." Trent must really be tired.

"The dumpster?"

"It was written in plain sight when he asked me questions."

"The DNA part?"

She cringed. "I was dusting in your house and cleaning up the papers, and the words jumped out at me. I couldn't miss them."

"Uh-huh. Just jumped out at you. What about the poison?"

Well, she didn't know that for sure until he just confirmed her suspicion. "I'll get to that. Stay with me. If I'm correct in thinking that last night was a copycat murder, then the murderer tried to replicate every last detail." Holly lifted the plate off the floor. "Cookie?"

"No thanks."

"The body was unharmed. No hits, stabs, or bullet wounds because there was no blood. I didn't see any sign of trauma to the head or marks on the neck from strangulation. Though, if it weren't poison, it might've been suffocation. If this followed the blueprint of the previous murders, then I'm assuming there were no obvious injuries with them either. Another factor that points to poison. It's probably not someone they knew unless somehow all the victims are connected…" She glanced to see if he'd reveal whether she was right or wrong. "Oh."

Trent had leaned his head against the wall, eyes closed, and his breathing had deepened. Asleep.

"Trent?" she whispered. "Let's get you home."

***

THE NEXT MORNING, after a fitful night's sleep, Holly sat in the window, Muffins at her feet. He seemed disgruntled that he had to share his new favorite spot. It was 6:30 a.m., and as usual, the line for *The Pie Crust* was ten-people long and growing by the minute.

She should just give in and visit the bakery. Find out what the big fuss was about. Shelly, her neighbor, had suggested there was more to it than just tasty treats. Right now, she studied and deduced information about people as they waited in line. It had been her experience with Teddy and his family—and Teddy's most recent attempt to force her to marry him after he'd framed her family—that she'd concluded she needed to read people better. For years, she'd been friends with Teddy. How could she not see the underlying control freak? Obviously, all too easily. That question still haunted her. She'd promised never to be in the position again. Plus, the skill of observation and reading body language would've helped in all the murders she'd helped solve.

People-watching didn't require a college degree. Just practice.

For example, a man stood halfway through the line. He shifted back and forth from one foot to the other. He constantly changed his arm positions. They were folded across his chest one minute, and the next he jammed them into his pockets. Then back to folded. Then tugging his mustache. Then at his sides, fingers drumming his pants. He was anxious or impatient. Maybe he woke late and had hoped to be first in line. Maybe he was afraid his favorite pastry would be gone.

For fun, Holly whipped out her notebook. Time to practice.

Yes, the man could just be impatient but everyone else would be too. It had to be something more. Problems with a woman. Problems at work. Maybe with his boss asking too much of him, putting on pressure.

Peering through the binoculars, Holly observed more closely. He was muttering. That was odd, because there were so many people around to hear him. Then she studied the man in front of him. Every few seconds, without looking back, the man talked. And then, the first guy responded.

Ah, they were having a hushed argument. Maybe they knew each other. Clearly, they didn't want to have this argument so were acting like they weren't. Oh, to stand behind them in line to confirm her theories.

Just as Holly moved onto the exhausted mother at the front of the line, a truck blocked her view. A moving truck! Furniture!

Holly rushed to her room and dressed, then met the men on the street. She introduced herself, let the movers know her apartment number, and then, begrudging, but curious, stood in line at *The Pie Crust*.

Her curiosity grew as the line steadily moved forward. She laughed as she found herself tapping her fingers and folding her arms. Okay, she could admit that there was always the possibility of reading too much into a situation or a person's body language.

She turned her thoughts to the owner of *The Pie Crust*. Obviously, people loved her. Holly envisioned a bright, eager smile, someone adorable, or at least presenting herself that way through a cheery personality and friendliness. An encouraging word as she—or he—accepted payment and sent a happy customer on their merry way. Decor and design said a lot about a person. And just based on the cute sign, Holly couldn't wait to see the inside of the place.

She wasn't disappointed.

The scent of cinnamon and sugar greeted her. She couldn't stop the smile for it reminded her of *Just Cheesecake*. The nostalgia memories hit. She refocused on the interior of the bakery. High circular tables were crammed into the shop. Several people stood around each one, chatting and eating.

Holly went on tiptoes to see above heads to the person behind the counter, which may or may not be the owner. Her jaw dropped in shock.

8

Holly tried her best not to judge on appearances. In fact, often, first impressions were wrong. As she'd learned the hard way. Sometimes there was beauty behind the beast. Right? Or was that just in fairy tales?

The woman behind the counter was…well, there was only one way to describe her. Large. Flaming red hair that could only be dyed, as gray roots showed. Triple chins. An image of Jabba the Hut appeared in Holly's mind. The woman's makeup was over-the-top: bright red lipstick, pink rouge, blue eyeshadow. Why in the world would someone apply makeup like that?

A couple approached the counter.

"Speak up!" the large woman rasped out.

"A blueberry muffin and two coffees. One black, one with cream and sugar," the man said loudly and with a touch of annoyance.

"Hey, everyone! A customer thinks he can be rude and shout at ole Junie Bug." The woman sneered at the customers.

Everyone in line booed.

"What do you say?" the woman who called herself Junie Bug taunted.

An older teen girl scurried in the background gathering the orders. She worked hard, her face tired but determined.

The couple mumbled.

"Speak up, I said, Or no…" Junie Bug motioned to the crowd.

"No service for those who don't listen to the Junie Bug!" everyone said together.

Junie Bug held back their order, waiting.

Finally, after an elbow nudge from the woman, together, the couple said, "Thank you to the Great Junie Bug!"

Begrudgingly, Junie Bug handed over their order, and the next person stepped up in the line.

Holly was fascinated. How did someone get away with such rudeness? How did this obnoxious woman create such a cute shop? Most customers would never return after being humiliated and mocked.

"What's that?" asked Junie Bug. "You know what happens when customers mumble."

This time it was a heavyset older woman. She spoke louder without shouting. "Low fat cinnamon scone, please."

Junie Bug chuckled, chins wobbling and her giant chest jiggling. "Trying to diet, huh? Good luck with that." Junie Bug grabbed and shook her massive stomach rolls. "But don't lose weight for any man or because you think it will make you happy. Find a man who loves you for who you are."

The woman nodded and paid for her order. "Thank you to the Great Junie Bug." Then she scurried out the door.

Holly grew more anxious as she moved up in the line. What kind of comment would this lady make about her?

Angry voices rose above the chatter and chaos. Two men stood, face-to-face. Mouths twitched and muscles tensed. At once, Holly recognized the man with the mustache as the one she'd been analyzing. His nervous behaviors had morphed into fury. The previous hushed conversation had erupted. Inevitably, she found herself leaning forward, listening.

"The blueberry tea bread definitely has lemon it." The man's mustache twitched.

The second man puffed his chest. "Do you dare argue with me? I was a pastry chef in my early years."

"Well, clearly, it was your very, very early years," the first man scoffed, a bit of spit landing on the chin of his opponent.

The second man wiped it off, spluttering.

While the men huffed and puffed, sorting their thoughts, Holly took a moment for her own speculation. Why in the world were they fighting about blueberry tea bread? Is that what they had been talking about while in line? The energy in the room skyrocketed, charged with tension. The room fell silent, everyone on their toes, anticipating a fight.

The second man's fists clenched into balls at his side. "You have done nothing but nitpick everything I've said from the moment you stood behind me in line! It's called polite conversation, if you didn't know. I was not looking for a formal debate on everything from the weather to men's dress shoes to pastries."

"What?" the first man cried. "You insult my intelligence!" He held up his fists. "Let's settle this. Man to man."

"Oh, no!" a raspy voice interrupted. Junie Bug moved from around the corner and waddled toward the men. "No fighting in *The Pie Crust*!" She stepped between them. She chuckled. "Unless you're fighting about which pastry is the best, right, guys?" She winked and nudged the man with the mustache.

He didn't respond but cast a dark look her way. The second man forced a laugh.

Junie Bug clapped. "Jay!" she screeched.

Seconds later, a thin man, with a familiar flop of graying hair, came from back in the kitchen. An apron hung from his neck. If the woman was large, this man was the complete opposite. "Yeah, June? Whaddya want?"

"This man has been extremely rude. Please escort him outside."

Jay darted forward, grabbed the man's arm, twisted it behind his back, and pushed him through the throng of people.

"B-but I've been waiting in line forever!"

Junie Bug waggled a finger. "Then you laugh when Junie Bug laughs. No fighting. Try again tomorrow, Clyde Peeling."

Soon, the man was gone, and Holly was amazed at how fast the tension dissipated. Maybe she hadn't been wrong about this guy. To lose his temper over pastry meant something else festered beneath the surface. She'd never know. Not that she would've asked.

Lost in her thoughts, a raspy voice snapped her back to the present. "You going to stand there all day, Missie?"

Holly stared into the face of Junie Bug. Gosh, she couldn't speak too loud or soft. And what was it they'd said after receiving their orders? Thank you, O most high, Junie Bug. No, that wasn't it.

"Spit it out. We've got customers." She looked beyond Holly. "Someone arrived at the counter and didn't know what they wanted!"

A chorus of boos sounded behind Holly. She said the first thing that came to mind. "Cheesecake. Please. To go."

Junie Bug paused, and her eyes narrowed. They weren't any special color, an almond brown, but there was a keen look to them, almost as if she could see right through

Holly. Like she knew her name, her family, and her history. She leaned across the counter, fat rolls flopping onto the wood. For the first time she spoke so softly, Holly could barely hear. "Are you sure about that? Once you try mine, you'll never want another."

Shivers spread across Holly's shoulders. The woman said one thing but her eyes said another, teasing Holly. A thought shot through her mind. No. Impossible! This woman could not know her name and business plans. Holly straightened. "I'll risk it."

Junie Bug slammed her hand down onto the counter. "We've got a live one, folks!" She held back the boxed cheesecake, waiting.

Holly's palms itched. Her mouth went dry. The words came at the last second. "Thank you to the Great Junie Bug!"

A broad smile spread across the woman's face as she focused on the next person in line.

Knees weak, Holly stumbled from *The Pie Crust*. She made her way across the street and sat on the bench. This might turn out to be her favorite spot. That was unlike any bakery, restaurant, place of business she'd ever experienced. That woman had her patrons trained, like mice in a maze.

They booed and cheered and responded practically on command. While reliving the experience and getting herself worked up, she opened the box and took a bite of the cheesecake. The flavors burst in her mouth. It was smooth. It was creamy. It was the perfect amount of sweet. How could a cheesecake taste this good?

Holly slumped. How would she ever compete?

She finished every last bite and scraped the bottom. She tossed the flattened box into the trashcan and realized the movers had left. She had a couch, a chair, a television, and a bed! Now, all she had left were the remaining boxes in her car.

Shrugging off the experience, and her downward spiraling thoughts, Holly rushed upstairs. The door was open a crack and a man's voice echoed from within. He was shushing Muffins. She hesitated outside the door. So far, her arrival had not gone as planned. In fact, it had been one mishap after another. She stormed into the room and came face-to-face with the intruder.

"You!" she said.

"Me? What are you doing here?" Detective Howe accused.

"Excuse me. I live here." She glared. "How did you get in here?"

"The movers were just leaving, so I was gracious and helpful enough to bring up the rest of your boxes."

The man was off-duty; in khaki shorts and a polo, he appeared to be more human, less intimidating. Even his black hair was mussed. Sweat dotted his brow. Holly studied the room. All the boxes from her car had been brought up to the apartment. Had Trent ordered him over here? That was the last thing she wanted.

Howe recovered quickly. He sank into the couch, making himself at home. "Hope you don't mind. This was my only time off."

"No. Not at all." She nodded. "Thank you for bringing up the boxes."

Silence fell between them, as they sized each other up. Holly's inner radar went off, encouraging her to use this situation to glean information on the dead man. Would they know anything this soon? Did Howe know she knew Trent yet?

He coughed. "I'm parched. If you could spare a glass of iced tea? Water?"

"Oh right." She poured him a glass of water. She supposed this was the time to offer some of the chocolate chip cookies she'd made, but she held back. Instead, she walked over to the window and sat. Muffins curled up on her lap. Before she could ask a question, he did.

"Have you fully recovered from the shock?"

"The shock of finding you in my apartment? Not really."

Howe didn't respond back with a quip, instead seemed to be giving her time. "Yes, well, when Wilkins asked me the other day to help him out, I came as fast as I could." He added, "Considering my work."

Wilkins? Who was that?

"Wilkins seemed troubled over his neighbor. Called her a troublemaker. Don't worry, he always has me help them move in so I can check them out."

Holly connected the dots. Wilkins was the man next door, and Howe was his godson. "Yes, well he seems to be quite the crotchety old man."

This wasn't the conversation she wanted to have, exchanging quips and subtle insults. She wanted information. She lowered her head, blinking. "I'll be honest. Even with all my Law & Order reruns, nothing prepared me for seeing the body. Do you ever get used to that? I mean, seeing bodies?"

He crossed his legs, assuming an even more casual pose. "No. And I hope I never do."

"Did you find out the man's name?" Holly held back the flood of questions she wanted to ask. Like what was the official cause of death? Did they agree with her that this murder was unrelated to the other ones?

He laughed.

"What?" Holly asked, defensive.

"Oh, nothing." He drained the glass of water. "Might as well tell you. The man's name was Daniel Croaker. A respected businessman in the community." He stopped there, as if he knew more but was waiting for something. "I'm surprised with your sleuthing skills you hadn't already figured that out."

Holly was shocked the man told her anything. "I didn't know him." She motioned to the boxes. "As you can see, I just moved in."

"Yes, I see that, Sherlock." He stood and stretched. "Welcome to town. Hope I don't receive any calls about noise complaints. I'm sure Wilkins will let me know if you're up to anything." He nodded. "Good day." Then he left.

The nerve of that man. Holly still felt like she'd given more away about herself than intended. That somehow, she'd been on trial. That he was the one questioning and then studying her body language. She also felt a bit silly about the night before when she gave him her analysis of the body. He was not a beat cop. He was a full-fledged detective.

Time to do a little detective work on her own. She had a few minutes before she had to be at the station to give her statement. The events of last night felt ages ago. Thankfully, with Howe off duty, she could talk to Trent.

9

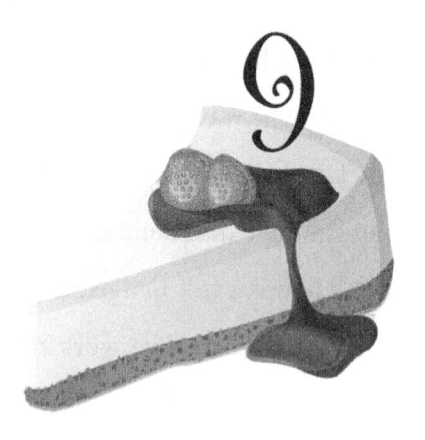

WITH CHEESECAKE ON the mind, Holly headed straight to the kitchen and mixed the ingredients. The decadent flavor of her competition still lingered in her memory. Maybe she just hadn't eaten cheesecake for a long time. Maybe the adrenaline rush the customers experienced inside *The Pie Crust* made the food taste better. Maybe…and she hated to admit this, maybe her cheesecake wasn't as good as she thought. Opening a business in a larger suburban area was more competitive than in a small town.

While the cheesecake baked, Holly showered and dressed in white capris and a pink ruffled tank. She spritzed perfume and walked into the mist, not wanting the scent to overpower the interrogation room, but considering she'd seen Trent at a crime scene and then he fell asleep on her, she wanted to make an impression.

She pulled into the police station. The brick building didn't seem any softer or more welcoming. "It's now or never."

This time, she strode to the desk and tapped her fingernail on the wood. "I'm here to give a statement to Chief Trinket." That's right. Sound confident.

The desk cop led her to the same interrogation room. "Wait in there. He'll be with you in a second."

Left alone in the room again, Holly closed her eyes and focused on the previous night, finding the body and recalling the details. She tried, to no avail, to recall the phone conversation she'd overheard in the grocery store. Something told her it was important but the words were gone.

The door opened and closed. To her dismay, she found herself in the company of Detective Howe again. He had a smirk like he knew way more than he let on. That he knew she expected Trent. His hair was combed and his uniform was spotless. Did this guy do anything for fun?

Probably read cold case files, or reviewed his past solved cases.

"Here we are again." He held out his hand, unsmiling. "I don't think we've officially met. I'm Detective Mason Howe."

Hesitantly, she shook his hand. "Holly."

"Holly…?"

"Hart." Might as well stick with that. Maybe no one would make the connection between Hart and Hartford.

"Right." He sat and opened his file to study the notes. "Start at the beginning. Tell me everything, for the record, about Daniel Croaker. How long have you known him?"

"Less than two days. But I didn't really know him. I'd just bumped into him a couple times."

"What was your first impression of him?"

"He was disgruntled. Angry. He told me he'd been threatened after exiting *The Pie Crust*." She took a breath. "Later, in the grocery store, he was still upset. I haven't been able to remember the exact phone conversation, because at the time I didn't realize he would be killed, but the tone was tense. He was tense." She tried again to bring up the words and couldn't. "He sounded defensive. Maybe you should look at his phone records. If he runs a business, talk to his clients."

"Should we talk to his family, too? What do you think?" Howe kept his eyes on his notes.

Holly assumed he'd be studying her reactions and body language. If he took offense at her suggestion, he didn't show it. His expression remained calm and controlled. Of course, they were looking at the guy's phone records.

"Did you have reason to dislike Daniel Croaker? Any business interactions with the man?"

She knew this detective didn't like her. Under different circumstances, like a party where Trent introduced her properly, Holly had the feeling he still wouldn't like her. His last question felt off. Like he thought she was a suspect. She didn't like it one bit. She was here to help.

"Please answer the question," he stated.

"Absolutely not. I'd just met the man."

He lifted his gaze from his notes, his eyes cold and penetrating. He pounced. "Yet you said that from the start the man was angry and off balance. Perhaps that had something to do with you?"

Holly felt her heart rate increase. "As I have already said, he was angry before he ever met me."

The detective leaned forward, his words sharp and piercing. "Maybe you are conveniently leaving out parts of the conversation. The parts that would make you look suspect."

"I'm not." She reflected his cold demeanor.

"And yet you coincidentally stood behind the man at the grocery store to overhear"—he made quotes with his fingers on his last word—"a conversation that would cast blame on someone else."

Holly gaped.

"I don't believe in coincidence, Ms. Hart." He quickly shifted to another question. "Tell me more about finding the body."

Feeling prickly but trying to cooperate, Holly recounted what she'd already told them, leaving to throw away boxes and then spotting the man's arm.

"Most people don't analyze the trash bins before throwing in their bags. Why didn't you recycle? Maybe because you hadn't lived in your apartment long enough to accumulate trash but needed an excuse to visit the dumpster. Maybe you called in the murder, then visited the dumpster as to look innocent."

"That's ridiculous and you know it. Anyway, you should hear my dog barking in the background of my phone call." Holly refused to sit in the seat of suspicion, so she turned the tables even knowing it was foolhardy. At this point, she didn't care. "Have you considered yet that this latest murder is different than the previous three? Do you see that most of the elements line up, except for the call-in?"

"Yes, and I find it interesting that you seem to be very wrapped up in this most recent one. Maybe you had an old score to settle and took advantage of the serial murders." He went back to studying his notes.

Holly's gaze followed his to the file. She was so mad she could barely focus. This man, who called himself a detective, was basing his conclusions on absolutely nothing but theories he'd invented in his own depraved mind. He was desperate. "Do you accuse all your witnesses of murder, Officer Howe?"

"That's Detective."

"Well, do you? It's highly unprofessional."

He feigned shock. "Why, Ms. Hart, I'm doing my job, considering all angles, all the people involved, the witnesses included. Maybe you should watch reruns of Castle or Miss

Marple to understand the field better. Consider it a helpful hint. Free of charge." He leaned back, his smirk reappearing.

She stood. "Are we done here? Or do you have any other questions?" she asked, sweetly.

"You may leave. But stay in town in case I need to follow up."

She strode to the door, trying to contain her fury and humiliation. Tears threatened but she refused to give into them. Her hand on the knob, he spoke again.

"I do have a follow-up question. I almost forgot. Earlier you'd mentioned he preferred his hot dog with no condiments. Did you observe this in action? Had you been stalking him? Or maybe you and he had dined previously before you officially moved to town."

Holly didn't turn back but said through clenched town. "No."

"Okay. Just checking. That's it."

She barely kept it together leaving the station and heading to her car. She refused to break down because he was probably watching to find some kind of perverse pleasure in her tears. Blinking fast, and not bothering to check for Trent's car, she drove from the lot, went about two miles, and then pulled over and gave in to the sobs. It wasn't just that he subtly and then not so subtly revealed her suspect status. It was the way he did it. He thoroughly mocked her previous observations. Poking fun at her reading into Daniel's personality through his actions. She slammed her fist against the wheel. "That jerk!" It was a completely valid method of detective work. And now, as the tears subsided, exhaustion settled over her. Time to go home.

For now, she'd rest in the fact that she left the station with one very important piece of information that would come in handy if needed.

Croaker's address.

***

HOLLY ARRIVED HOME, wiped out, but with one more item on her list to accomplish. Cheesecake in hand, she knocked on her neighbor's door. For being a grumpy old man, he certainly had heart. Why else would he ask his godson—who unfortunately turned out to be Howe—to help with the boxes? With this kind of personality, one had to be patient.

No one answered the door.

Holly knocked again. This time with more force. Was he not home or was he ignoring her? She pressed her ear to the wood. Nothing. She knocked again, and listened. Should she leave the cake in the hall with a note?

Without notice, the door opened. Holly fell forward. Stumbling, she quickly adjusted and came face to face with him. "Oh, hi." She waved and smiled.

He leaned on his cane, staring in an unfriendly manner.

She lifted the cheesecake. "I made a cake for you." He still didn't respond, so she rambled. "A way to say thank you. Your godson was quite helpful earlier today." Balancing the cake on her left arm, she stuck out her hand. "I'm Holly."

He snorted. "I know all about you, Holly Hart."

Taken aback, Holly wasn't sure what to say to that. "Oh."

Finally, he shook hands. "Sam Wilkins." He eyed the cake. "Is it soft? My teeth aren't what they used to be, you know."

"Yes, very smooth and soft."

He shuffled back. "You can put it on the table."

Holly entered and was surprised at the cleanliness and order of his apartment. What did she expect? Maybe a pile of dishes in the sink. Piles of magazines. Or Jeopardy playing too loudly on the television.

He seemed to read her mind. "I know. Surprised that an old man likes a clean home, aren't you?"

"Um, not at all. I think it's wonderful." She backed toward the door, smiling.

"Liar."

Heat crawled up the back of her neck. "Again, thank you for enlisting the help of your godson." She didn't mean to but she grimaced just thinking about him.

Wilkins laughed and then coughed. "Yeah, I know he's a donkey's butt."

Normally, Holly would refute a statement like that but after her day with him, she couldn't muster the words.

"Don't worry. He doesn't like you either."

"Why? What did he say?" Holly asked, regretting it afterwards. Did she really want to know? It wasn't going to be anything nice.

"That you're a suspect in a murder case."

It was the question or the possible belief in the old man's eyes that rattled Holly. Fury spiked. "That's not fair. Just because I discovered the body last night, he assumed I could be guilty. He probably felt threatened by an intelligent female who saw more into the case than he had. Obviously, Daniel Croaker was a very particular but unsettled man.

Howe dismissed any of my thoughts. Why did he call me in if he planned on ignoring the evidence? He had the nerve to suggest that reading into personality to predict behavior was poor sleuthing and—"

"It is."

Holly gaped.

"That kind of nonsense doesn't hold up in court. Not that a smart detective doesn't think it, but facts are a necessity. And the fact remains that cops have to consider everyone involved in a murder. Including the witnesses."

"W-well, he also mocked and humiliated me when I gave my statement."

"Why do you think he did that?"

"He's sexist."

"Go deeper."

"He's insecure."

"Try again."

"He's a jerk." But Holly thought about it. Even if her analysis of Daniel Croaker wasn't on the up and up, as far as evidence, she still considered the insight worthy of consideration. She thought about cops and methods, and yes, TV shows. She deflated. "He was trying to shock me so

I'd slip up. So he could get past any facade I was trying to present."

Wilkins nodded. "I see you went over to the dark side." His point taken, he changed directions. When Holly didn't catch his meaning, he motioned toward the window.

"Oh, right." Holly thought back on her time in *The Pie Crust*, and all thoughts of the case left her mind, and the reality of her competition rushed in and took its place. Because thinking about the case for fun or to needle Howe didn't stack up against her future here. One weighed more on her mind than the other.

"You going to stick around here until dinner, or what?"

His words snapped Holly from her reverie. He must've used up his niceness for the day. Or it was time for Jeopardy. "Sorry. Just thinking."

When Holly was at the door, he spoke again. "Funny thing. Before *The Pie Crust*, there was another bakery." He smacked his lips. "They made great cupcakes. Not too sweet. Anyway, they had to close shop because of a rat infestation."

10

THE NEXT DAY, RESTLESS, and feeling like she should be doing something about starting her business, Holly went to the library. After a good night's sleep and putting Howe out of her mind, she was ready to form a business plan. But Wilkins' last words about a rat infestation closing the competition made her curious. What kind of bakery was able to compete with *The Pie Crust*? Outside of the whole rat thing were they successful?

She wanted to know more.

Of course, the library visit had nothing to do with the fact that the archived newspapers would also hold information on the serial murders. She had a strong suspicion it would be impossible to get any information from Trent. If she ever spent time with him. The new job of Chief of Police was time consuming. She knew that but the reality of not seeing him was much harder than expected.

Holly stopped at the computers first. She typed in the terms *dumpster deaths* and *serial murders*. She skimmed articles searching for facts about the murders she didn't know. Her bruised ego could use a boost too, especially after both Howe and Wilkins shot down her theories.

Several articles confirmed what she already knew.

No DNA.

No evidence.

Murder happened off sight. Poison.

No prominent suspects—at least that they shared with the newspapers.

No connections, yet, between the murder victims.

And all the bodies had been discovered by various people, completely by accident. In other words, no call-ins.

She was right that this most recent murder wasn't connected to the others. She let her mind explore the possibilities. Clearly, the serial murderer was a perfectionist, a planner, and knew something about forensics. He or she could possibly be a cop or a scientist. Or a pharmacist, to know enough about poisons. This most recent murder, the man or woman was also smart, copying the serial murders. Having exhausted the available information and satisfying her curiosity, Holly moved on to find something about the bakery closing and the rat infestation.

As she suspected, the bakery closing hadn't made the papers. There was nothing morbid or all that interesting about a failed business. It happened all the time.

"Holly, is that really you?"

About time. This was the reason Holly had used the computers at the library. She needed someone to answer questions. The librarian was the perfect choice. Holly had attended high school with Katie Carter. Katie had graduated valedictorian. She was extremely intelligent but lacked common sense. This gave her the special ability to think outside the box. And, to recall details.

Holly turned. "Katie!" She stood and hugged her acquaintance. They hadn't been best buds but still knew each other fairly well. Katie looked the same, except a few pounds heavier. Shoulder-length dark blonde hair, warm smile, friendly. Still beautiful. "Been on Jeopardy yet?"

"Not yet. Too busy. But one of these days."

"I'm surprised you ended up back in town." Katie had been the one destined for world travel or life in a big city.

Katie lost her smile. "Life doesn't always work as planned. After my dad fell ill, he needed help around the house. I didn't feel like I should move away. He's better now, but I love my job."

"Family is more important. I admire your choice. And I understand about job security." Holly hesitated, unsure how to spark the conversation naturally. She might as well be honest. "I was wondering if you could help me with something."

Katie sat at the next computer. "What do you want to know?" Her eyes were bright as if the chance to help or share knowledge thrilled her.

"Have you been to *The Pie Crust*?" Holly asked.

"Gosh, yes. Of course. Everyone has. Isn't June a hoot?"

"You mean the Great Junie Bug?"

"Ah, so I see you've been. That's her nickname. Her full name is June Marsh. What did you think?" Katie asked.

"Um, it was interesting."

"You'll get used it." Katie laughed. "I promise. Next thing you know you'll look forward to it. The experience is unpredictable."

"I heard their only competitors went out of business," she said, lightly.

"Yes, it was ghastly business." Katie tapped her fingers on the table. "It was six months ago." She leaned forward and whispered, "Rats!"

Ugh. Rats. "But rats shouldn't close a business."

Katie leaned forward and tapped the keys of Holly's computer. "It was more than that. It was a full-out smear campaign. The rat infestation was the straw that closed the bakery. You know what I mean. And when I say smear campaign, I mean brutal. Everything from stealing recipes to adultery to poor business practices. All gossip and lies. Ah, here it is."

The paper appeared on the screen. A title screamed across the top of the article. Local Business Closes Due to Rat Plague! Holly forwarded the article to her email so she could study it later.

"Why so interested?" Katie asked.

"I plan on opening a bakery, and I want to know what I'm up against," Holly admitted.

"Good luck with that. Any way I can help, just ask. I'd better get back to the desk."

"One more thing, Katie."

"Sure, anything."

"What do you know about Daniel Croaker?"

Katie tapped her chin. "Daniel Croaker. That name sounds familiar."

"He was murdered and found in a dumpster the other night." Holly supplied the information and eagerly waited for Katie's response.

Katie didn't even blink at the word murder. "Yes, but that's not it. I remember seeing the name before. Grr." She screwed up her face in thought but then just as quickly brushed it off. "It'll come when I'm not thinking about it. When I'm shelving books or something like that."

"How about I give you my number and you can text me later if you remember." Holly pulled out her phone.

"You mean when I remember. I always remember, and I never forget. Just temporarily misplace the information in my mind." Katie entered her number into Holly's contacts. "We should get together for lunch. Talk about the old times, and gossip." She winked. "I'd love to hear the story behind your parents and… your involvement in that whole sordid affair. How exciting."

"I'm not sure exciting is quite the word." Holly would rather forget her parents having to disappear for their own safety. Except, without that happening Holly never would've opened *Just Cheesecake* or met Trent, Charlene, and Millicent.

Katie eyed Holly with suspicion. "Doing a little sleuthing, huh?"

"Something like that. Where was the bakery located that had problem with rats?"

"Walk about half a mile down from *The Pie Crust*. It's now a pharmacy. Let me know if I can be of help." She stood. "I'd better get back to work."

***

MUFFINS WOULD MAKE THE perfect partner for her next mission, and he could use the walk. She hooked on the leash. "Okay, let's go."

The past few days had been packed with events, new people, and information. Her mind was reeling. She could forget about Daniel Croaker for a bit, let that case simmer in the background. There really weren't any leads to follow. She didn't have a list of relatives to question. The police would never let her look at the phone records. Honestly, she didn't know much about the man except for the few things she'd deduced, and no one cared about that. So, with that murder on the back burner she could focus on her business. Research. Research. Research.

Soon, she was at the pharmacy. The door jingled above her head as it closed. She approached the checkout counter. A middle-aged woman appeared bored from her expression and lack of enthusiasm. "May I help you?"

"Yes, in fact you can. Is the owner available?"

"Wait just a minute." The woman went back between the aisles and disappeared from sight.

Holly took in the store and tried to envision it as a bakery. Hmm. A lot must've been done to turn it into a pharmacy. Though with a vivid imagination, Holly was able to envision it. Location was so important for a business, especially in the food industry.

A young man approached. "Yes, I'm the owner. Patrick Young."

Holly pasted on a warm smile. "Yes, hello. I'm new to the neighborhood and…will soon be opening a business. I'm checking in with a few of the business owners in town.

I'd heard about the rat infestation about six months ago. Do you still have any problems with rats?"

He sniffed and acted insulted. "Absolutely not." Then he said, quietly, "I expected to pay a lot for pest control, but when they arrived they couldn't find any rats. They'd vanished." He smiled. "Lucky on my part."

No rats? "That's odd." Rats didn't usually up and leave without a reason. "Did you know anything about the bakery that closed down?"

"Only that the guy was furious."

"Do you know his name, by any chance?" Holly asked.

"Charles, I think. Yes, Charles Brally."

"Do you know if he still lives in the area?"

"No idea. Now if you don't mind." He nodded and then went back to work.

Holly tugged on Muffins' leash. "Let's go." At home, she texted Trent about dinner at his place tonight. Seconds later, he texted back. *Yes.*

She now knew her next mission. Romance.

11

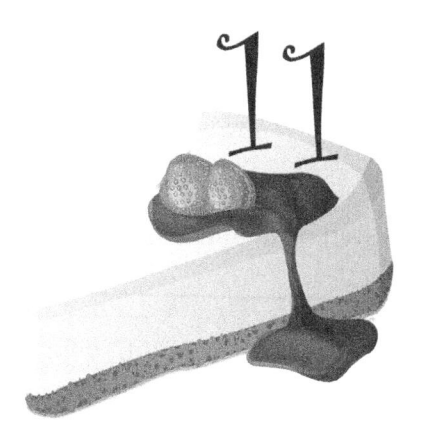

Holly only had to search Pinterest for romantic date ideas but most of them were too cutesy or would take too much planning. Dinner together, alone, with a glass of wine, soft music, and conversation would be perfect. And with Trent's work schedule and job stress, he probably wouldn't mind being at home.

She bustled about her apartment gathering supplies for a simple meal of spaghetti and meatballs and garlic bread.

Muffins yipped by the door, a classic puppy-dog look on his face.

"Oh, you want to come, do you?" In the past couple days, she'd only taken Muffins on walks. Other than that, he'd been locked in the apartment. "Fine, you'll join us tonight."

Muffins seemed to understand and dragged the leash over to Holly.

"Okay, okay. I get the point." First, she loaded the supplies into her car and then returned for Muffins. "Let's get cooking!"

In Trent's apartment, she freed Muffins, who immediately curled up on the couch. She got to work in the kitchen. Trent wasn't home yet, but hopefully he would be soon. Instead of another no-show. With the sauce simmering and the pasta ready to plop in when Trent arrived, Holly thought about Katie Carter. They hadn't been the best of friends in high school, but Holly saw a lot of potential in a future friendship. Honestly, Holly didn't have many requirements. Just someone who was looking for friendship too. And, it didn't hurt that she seemed excited about a little sleuthing adventure.

Holly didn't hear the door open and close until Trent's footsteps sounded behind her.

"You seem lost in thought," he said, teasing. "Let me guess. You're analyzing all the clues you've racked up so far, real or imaginary."

She turned and feigned shock. "Excuse me! My clues are never imaginary." Her neighbor's words ran through her mind. "Can I ask you something?"

"Maybe..." He raised an eyebrow. In other words, she could ask but he might not answer.

"Don't worry. I know the murder case is off limits. I have a police procedural question."

"Not sure I'll answer that either. I don't want to give you any ideas." He lifted the saucepot lid and sniffed. "Hmm. Smells delicious."

Holly eased the pasta into the boiling water. "So..." What was the best way to put this without sounding silly? "When you're investigating a case, do you ever read into a person's body language and temperament?" She held up a finger to let him know she wasn't done. "And then use that to investigate in a certain direction?"

He leaned against the counter. "We're speaking hypothetically, of course. Right?"

"Of course. For example, hypothetically"—she emphasized the last word—"if a witness through his or her observations makes a relevant suggestion, should, or would, a detective take it seriously?"

"What do you think?" he asked, softly.

She stirred the pasta and lowered the heat. "I think, at first, the detective might not like that a citizen knew more than him but that eventually he might consider it." She laughed. "Obviously, not as evidence to arrest someone on the spot."

"I see you've given this a lot of thought."

She shrugged. "Just a question I had and you've been busy."

He sighed and opened his arms. "Come here."

With a quick intake of breath, Holly melted into his embrace, his warmth. She breathed in his scent. It hit her how much she'd missed him, missed this. Since her arrival they hadn't even had a proper hug.

"Are you sniffing me?" He laughed.

"Um…yes?"

"You should at least wait until I'm out of the shower."

"Oh, don't worry. You smell yummy." She always loved the lingering scent of Old Spice, along with a hint of police station coffee.

"Yummy? Now that's not a scent I've ever seen in a store."

"It should be." She closed her eyes and enjoyed the feeling of safety. The last few days had been unsettling. "You know you haven't even kissed me yet," she murmured.

"Well, let's correct that." He pulled away and lifted her face with his finger. His gaze dropped to her mouth and he kissed her.

She sighed into the kiss. She could stay here forever and might've if the boiling water hadn't caught her attention. One peek and the sight of the foam said it was about to boil over. "Hold that thought." She drained the pasta.

"How about we skip dinner?" Trent tugged on the back of her shirt.

"We'll save the smooching for later."

Together, they prepared the meal and sat at his table for two. She decided not to press for an answer to her question, which he'd conveniently not answered.

"Have you contacted a realtor yet?" he asked, spaghetti dangling from his mouth.

The giggle about to escape died at the mention of a realtor. *The Pie Crust*, more specifically, the owner, left her conflicted. "I have a couple in mind."

"What's wrong?" He wiped his mouth, smirking. "I expected more excitement."

Suddenly, the pasta on her plate was fascinating.

"Talk to me," he prodded.

She fought back the tears as the discouragement she'd been holding off rushed back. "Have you been to *The Pie Crust*?"

"Ah yes. The Great Junie Bug. Who hasn't? She's infamous."

"Exactly. I'll never be able to compete with her obnoxious approach to treating customers." She winced just thinking about it.

"Competition is a good thing." He spoke more softly. "Right?"

"I realize that but…" She thought back on what she'd learned at the library and the previous bakery closing, and what Katie had shared. "Did you know that six months ago the other bakery closed? Supposedly due to a rat infestation, but then Katie at the library told me someone launched a smear campaign against the owner. And then, I talked to the new business owner and he said there never were any rats. What if June orchestrated it all to shut down the competition? And if she did, what will that mean for me? She could dig up plenty on my past here in town and—"

"Holly!"

She fell silent.

His expression softened. "You haven't had an easy welcome to town, have you?"

"Not really." Her voice cracked with emotion.

"I'm sorry I haven't been here for you."

"You have this big case and the stress of your new job. I understand." It still felt nice to hear.

He leaned back in his chair. "Alright, let's look at the evidence. Do you have hard evidence on June Marsh, or…are you reading into behaviors and making a conclusion?"

Darn him. "Fine. Point taken." She might not have hard evidence but it was still worth investigating as part of the ongoing research for her business. How she missed a bakery closing due to a rat infestation, she wasn't sure, but it was better to know exactly what happened. She decided to keep that to herself.

"On that note, how about ice cream?" he asked.

***

HAND IN HAND, they strolled Main Street. Muffins trailed, sniffing everywhere for the right place to pee. It was a beautiful evening and the warm breeze felt nice. Holly couldn't help but survey the crowds and think that surely not everyone enjoyed June's approach to customer service. Maybe Trent was right about competition being healthy.

"The Right Scoop is the best ice cream around." Trent motioned to the sign up ahead where a line was growing. "Guess we're not the only ones craving ice cream."

Someone waved frantically from the line. "Holly!"

"Who's that?" Trent asked as they neared the line.

"That's Katie. A friend from high school and the town librarian." She waved enthusiastically, her honey hair bouncing around her shoulders.

Trent nudged her. "See! You're already making friends.

She moved forward, smiling. "Hi, Katie!"

"You've got to join us. I insist. We can grab a table and chat." She eyed Trent. "Ooh, you landed the new chief for a date."

Holly noticed Trent's blush. "Actually, we were dating before he moved here." She held up her ring finger with the flashing diamond.

Katie gasped. "You should've told me. Congrats!" She hugged Holly then stepped back. "Meet my hunky boyfriend." She stepped aside. "Holly, this is Mason, and I guess the guys already know each other."

Trent nodded. "Mason."

Flabbergasted. That could only describe Holly's reaction. Muffins growled at him. "Y-you're dating Officer Howe?"

"Yup! Coming on two months next week. Do you know each other?" Katie asked.

Howe smirked. "You could say that. And that's Detective Howe."

"Right." Hopes of a friendship with Katie crashed and burned. How could she even stand to be around this guy? And how long did it take to eat ice cream so she and Trent could leave? And with Katie so interested in murder and mysteries, how was she dating a cop who detested citizen participation?

Katie hooked her arm through Mason's. "I sense a story there."

They ordered ice cream and found a seat. Katie jumped right into it. "So guys, update us on the latest murder case." She lowered her voice. "Any viable suspects?"

"You could say that," Mason answered, without smiling, his gaze flicking to Holly.

Holly stifled her disdain. What did Katie find attractive about this stiff, boring, strait-laced man? Katie was much too bubbly and enthusiastic for him. Though, Holly admitted he was attractive. Even more so if he ever smiled or displayed a personality.

Katie squeezed his hand. "Don't tease us. Give us some details. Any details."

Holly waved her hand and laughed. "Obviously, they can't share details of the case. So, what's there to do in the area? What are some good date nights?" She hated that she sounded breathless, nervous.

"Glad you think so, sweetie." Trent jumped into the conversation. "That we shouldn't share details of ongoing cases." He smiled, beaming with pride. "Actually, Holly is an accomplished amateur sleuth. Despite my disapproval. In Fairview, she'd end up smack dab in the middle of the investigation and played a key role in bringing suspects to justice."

"Really?" Mason asked, his gaze intensifying. "That's good to know."

Holly was aghast. If only she'd shared her miserable interactions with this man with Trent, then he'd know that's the last thing he should have said. Now, Howe would be onto her, suspect of everything she did.

Katie squealed. "That's so exciting. I see a girls' night in our near future where you tell me everything."

Holly sensed it coming and wanted to kick Katie under the table.

Katie babbled, "Never mind everything that happened here in town recently. With that creepy guy. What was his name?" she asked. "And then the chief was fired. It was all pretty exciting. No one thinks the chief of their town will be a bad cop. That's for movies."

"Definitely, the movies," Trent said.

"How about this ice cream?" Holly asked. "Mine's delicious." She fully expected a snarky comment from Mason, but instead, the opposite happened. He fell silent. Probably figuring out whether she should be pegged as a suspect or a meddling busybody. Or both. Forget innocent stop-ins at the station to visit Trent.

"So, guys," Katie persisted. "Any information you can spill?" She nuzzled up against Mason, and for the first time, a warm, affectionate smile brightened his expression.

When they didn't answer, Katie didn't let up. "Let's see. We'll guess, then. Won't we, Holly?"

"Um, sure." Absolutely not! She had no intentions of sharing any of her growing theories, so she let Katie ramble. Her enthusiasm was catchy.

"How about this?" Katie licked the side of her cone before a drop fell onto her dress. "The murder victim was about to receive an immense fortune, and a distant cousin, out of the blue, killed him for money. Or, this man had been collecting personal, embarrassing information on people in town. Then he started blackmailing them. Eventually, one of his victim's had enough and murdered him, stabbed him in the back and left him in a dumpster."

"Except there were no stab wounds." The words had slipped out. Holly quickly clammed up, not wanting to make the situation worse.

Howe pounced. "What do you think, Miss Hart?"

Holly shrugged. "I don't know. There's not enough hard evidence. I wouldn't want to bandy about thoughts based on observation. Where's the science behind that?"

Trent flashed her a confused look, obviously picking up on her underlying sarcasm and relating it to her earlier question.

Katie was only picking up steam. "Ooh, what if he had a mistress furious that he'd broken up with her. You know what they say? Most murder is about love or money."

Trent chuckled. "I guess we should have this case wrapped up in no time, then."

Everyone laughed except Detective Howe.

Holly nudged Trent. "I should get back."

"What the—?" Mason jumped up, his chair falling backward. "Your stupid dog peed on my foot."

Holly tugged on the leash. "Muffins, come back here." She pulled Muffins onto her lap. She wanted to say Good Dog, but used self-control. No need to make the situation worse.

Trent offered Mason napkins. "I guess that wraps up the evening."

Mason growled.

Katie slugged him. "Don't worry. We'll wash them up back at your house. They'll be good as new in the morning." She kissed his cheek then whispered in his ear. Immediately, Mason softened.

As they turned to leave, Katie cried out, "I remember!"

Trent and Holly turned. "What?" everyone said at the same time.

"About Daniel Croaker."

Terrific. Holly inwardly groaned. Why now? Why her? Trent and Mason went on alert, both interested in what Katie had to say.

"Oh, what's that?" Holly stroked Muffins, for comfort.

"He'd been the building inspector on that bakery. He was the one who found the rats and closed down the business."

12

THE NEXT MORNING, Holly nursed a cup of coffee while staring outside her window. She wasn't looking at anything specifically. Her mind was running at high speed. Finally, she had to empty it. She brought her mug to the kitchen sink and then grabbed a notebook and a pen. Just the sight of the gift basket brought a wave of homesickness for Charlene and the girls.

Katie sure had dropped a bomb to end the already explosive evening. Needless to say, good thing Holly had filled the drive to her apartment with shallow non-stop conversation. Trent had an early morning or she was sure he would've grilled her. In fact, she expected the inquisition to happen as soon as he had the time.

Trent and Howe must've already known Daniel Croaker's profession. But had they talked to Katie, and did they know about the smear campaign against Patrick Brally—owner of the closed bakery? Holly had the burning desire to solve the mystery before Detective Howe. Prove that she could rub brain cells together and come up with solid logic. Never mind prove her innocence.

She made a list.

1. Daniel Croaker found dead.

2. He was a building inspector.

3. He closed down at least one business under possible false pretenses. Maybe it wasn't the first time. Research? Hard evidence!!!! (Darn that Detective Howe!)

4. The man potentially had enemies.

5. Maybe he took bribes?

6. June Marsh could've paid him off to close the competition. Investigate!

She wasn't quite ready to jot down her next thought. What if June Marsh not only paid him off but then killed him because he was a loose thread?

***

TODAY WOULD BE A day of solid sleuthing. When Holly kicked her feet up at the end of the day, she'd have something of substance to write in her notebook. A real reason to cross off a suspect or circle a name.

Her plans called for a no-nonsense outfit, one that didn't draw too much attention or cast her as any kind of personality. Because everyone despite what they say judges a book by its cover. So khaki shorts and a blue and white striped shirt it would be.

Holly pulled up to Sky View Realty. Several minutes later she was still sitting in the car. Her confidence in her cheesecake and business plan had spiraled ever since she'd entered *The Pie Crust*. Festering under her skin was the question of the smear campaign. Most likely, another bakery that popped up would receive the same treatment, unless Holly figured out who was behind it. But, then again, it wouldn't hurt to at least check out potential properties.

A small woman sat behind the desk. Her hair was light brown, almost gray, and the way she nibbled at a rice cake reminded her of a mouse. Holly cleared her throat.

The woman jumped and tucked away her snack, smoothing her hair and shirt, and wiping off crumbs. "Yes, may I help you?"

Holly sat in the chair on the opposite side of the desk. "Yes, I hope you can. I'm new in town."

"Welcome," the woman said warmly, smiling.

"Thank you." Holly nodded. "I'm hoping to open a business." The woman pulled out a notepad to write the details. Holly continued, "I'm willing to wait for the right spot, too. But it wouldn't hurt to check out properties."

"Right. Definitely not. New businesses are always good."

"Are there any available on Main Street?" Holly asked, hating the hesitancy in her voice. June Marsh had played a number on Holly's mind, and she hated it.

The woman let out a squeak of a laugh, like it was ridiculous for Holly to even ask. "I'll pass on the information to the realtors. It might help to know what kind of business."

"Um." Holly bit her bottom lip. She knew the information would be helpful but if this secretary knew about *The Pie Crust* and the Great Junie Bug, then.... "A bakery, specializing in cheesecake, so I'd need a commercial kitchen or space for one."

"Oh." The woman's expression said it all.

Holly decided to play innocent. "Is there something wrong?"

"Well, no. Not really."

It would be wrong of any secretary to discourage clientele, but this woman had to know more. Holly laughed. "Honestly, I'm just testing the idea. Not even sure about the timeline. Are there many competing bakeries in the area?"

The woman nibbled on her nail. "How long have you been in town?"

"Only a couple days."

"Well, there is a bakery on Main Street. You should definitely check that one out. And there was another one but it closed last year."

Holly feigned innocence. "Do you know why it closed?" She pressed her hands to her chest. "I'm really in the research stage so it would be so helpful to know why or how they closed. Was the competition too steep? Not enough room for two bakeries? Or was it something else? Poor location? After all, location is extremely important, which was why I thought about Main Street. Do you know why it closed?"

The woman's eyes darted to the right and left. She leaned across the desk. "Rats!" she whispered.

Holly gasped. "Oh, that's terrible."

The woman shrugged. "Yes, it is. But they wouldn't have been open much longer. Business had been on the decline for weeks."

"Oh." Holly twirled a lock of hair around her finger. "Why?"

"Well, there were rumors." The woman hesitated again. "I'm not sure how much stock to put in the paper, but before the rats, the bakery had been accused of stealing recipes and just bad business practices. You know, poor customer service."

Holly had to stifle blurting out Ha! No one seemed to mind poor customer service in this town. "Where I lived before, the building inspector was very strict. Kitchens were about impossible to pass. It was ridiculous. Do you know any of the inspectors in town?"

The woman paled. "There was one that many of the businesses used." She bit her lower lip, then blurted, "He was murdered!"

"Murdered?" Holly let out a gasp.

"Yes, in a dark alley, at night, alone and vulnerable."

"Oh, gosh. Did he have any enemies?"

"I'm sure." The color returned to her face. "He had no mercy. Neither did his little sidekick. Plenty of business owners probably held a grudge against him. Were the grudges big enough for murder? I don't know. I mean, he almost had *The Pie Crust* closed down! Imagine that."

"Did the inspector have family or a girlfriend?"

"I don't think so." She giggled. "He wasn't well-liked. He'd have to move to get a date." She realized what she'd said. "Sorry. I don't like to speak ill of the dead."

"What about this smear campaign? I wouldn't mind knowing more about that. Were the rumors true?"

The woman shrugged. "Doesn't matter. People believed them." She once again looked about before speaking. "Really, you should ask the editor at the newspaper. He'll know more."

"I just might do that." Holly stood. "Do know his name?"

"Finnigan Shelton. His family has owned it for generations. Old money."

"Thanks."

It was time to leave. She left her name and number with the secretary, and after a polite thank you and goodbye, Holly left.

It wasn't hard to find the newspaper office tucked away behind a used clothing store in a nondescript building. She assumed their success was more in the presentation of their words than in the appearance of the work place. She pushed on the glass door and entered. She marched up to the desk and pressed the bell.

Within a minute, a man, glasses pushed up onto his head, hurried out. If this man was Mr. Shelton, he was much younger than Holly expected, much more flustered, and much more innocent-looking for someone who wrote hit pieces.

"So sorry. We're short-staffed today." He whipped out a notepad. "How can I help? Do you want to place an ad? You can purchase a quarter, half-page, full-page, in color or black and white."

"I'd like to speak with Finnigan Shelton, please."

He pulled his glasses down over his nose and studied her. "On what business?"

She cleared her throat as if she had something important to say. Holly had the feeling she wouldn't get through the layers of defense around the chief editor. "It's about the integrity of the paper."

He bristled. "Excuse me? Our integrity is just fine and dandy."

"I'm talking about the smear campaign that closed down a thriving business. Lies and gossip, allowed to be printed and spread by your own chief editor." Thriving might've been an exaggeration, as she didn't know much about the bakery before it closed its doors. "And"—she straightened, trying to add inches to her height—"as a potential business owner, I'd like to feel secure in the fact that the newspaper won't print scandalous stories that aren't true."

The once-confident man crumpled before her eyes. "You mean Henrietta Belch." He shook his head. "I should've realized it was a non de plume."

"Henrietta?" Holly asked.

He leaned on the counter. "I know the business you are referring to. Henrietta sent in op-ed pieces. I suppose you could call it a gossip column. I did away with it once I realized what happened. Some of the most severe lies were tucked in the middle of the piece. Lies that went unnoticed."

"That's what I'm talking about. Integrity. Now, may I talk to Mr. Shelton?"

He looked puzzled. "I'm Mr. Shelton. And I go by Finn."

Holly had to clench her jaw to keep it from dropping open. This Mr. Shelton, if she could take him at face value, didn't appear to have been in charge. "Did you realize this smear campaign happened right under your nose?"

"Sadly, no. Of course, looking back, in hindsight, I see it clearly."

"Did you ever meet this Henrietta Belch?" With a handy description, surely, Holly could find the guilty party. Especially if the description matched June Marsh's. She was unforgettable.

"Again, no. Everything was submitted my mail."

"Do you have an address or phone number?" Surely, he had to have something.

He offered a sad smile.

She grew desperate, even though realizing this was probably a dead end. "How about a return address on the envelope? Anything?"

"I wish. But no. I'm sorry I can't help you, but I wish you every success with your new business."

"Thanks."

The man hurried back behind the doors to work on next week's edition. Just a simple description would've ruled out June Marsh.

13

AFTER SHE'D TALKED TO the realtor and the editor, she dropped by the library, curious if Katie had any news. Or if Detective Howe had told her never to speak to Holly again. "What are we doing?"

"Isn't it obvious?" Katie giggled and grabbed Holly's arm, leading to a table tucked away in a corner. "We don't want anyone to hear us. Did anyone follow you?"

"I don't think so." Holly hadn't even thought to check. There had been no reason to suspect that. "I've been in that position before and I'm not really poking my nose into business that's not mine. Yet."

Katie raised an eyebrow. "My detective boyfriend would say otherwise."

"Great. Tell me." Holly knew it.

"After ice cream where I stupidly let him know you'd been asking about Daniel Croaker, he said a few things. I am so sorry. I had no idea about anything. You'd asked questions and everything but that's different than, you know."

Holly wasn't sure she wanted to know. "What?"

"Trying to scoop the cops? Sneaking around and trying to solve a murder?" Katie's expression held only enthusiasm, not judgment.

"I guess you could look at my actions like that, but I prefer to look at it as a future businesswoman planning and researching before opening day."

"How does Croaker play into that?"

"Well…"—Holly wasn't sure how much to share with Katie—"I'm not sure yet."

Katie leaned back in her chair, studying Holly, her gaze piercing. She hesitated, then said, "Liar. But I get it. Not everyone wants to be friends with a cop's girlfriend." She pouted. "I just figured you of all people would get that."

Holly sighed. "Detective Howe and I aren't exactly seeing eye to eye on anything. He insinuated I was a suspect, humiliated me, and dismissed my opinions."

"I know. He can be dreadful sometimes." She waved her hand. "That's the part of him that makes him a good detective though. He doesn't take anyone at face value, but he'll come around. Maybe."

Holly desperately wanted to trust her old but new friend. Someone to bounce ideas off. Sometimes, the unseen became more obvious during a conversation. "I can't have you telling him everything I tell you."

Katie made the sign of a cross over her chest. "Cross my heart and hope to die. I won't say anything. Now, what does your business have to do with Croaker's murder?"

Where to begin? Holly took a moment to think it all through: the different pieces, the various conversations she'd had, and what she'd observed. "What if June Marsh was trying to close down her competition and—"

"Ooh, ooh, I've got this. And paid off Croaker to make up the part about the rats!"

"Yes!" That was exactly it. "I went to the owner who purchased the bakery space, and he said there were never any rats."

"Very suspicious," Katie said. "What else?"

"Daniel Croaker had left *The Pie Crust* angry. He told me he'd been threatened—"

"By the Great Junie Bug!" Katie gasped. "Do you think the Junie Bug did him in? Maybe he'd been blackmailing her or she was trying to tie up loose ends."

"It's one theory."

"Ah, and you want to find out more before you attempt to open another bakery." Katie stood. "Makes perfect sense to me. Have you told Trent any of this?"

"Um, no. He's been busy."

"Okay, then let's go," Katie stated.

"Where?"

"To do some sleuthing!" Katie cried.

"Shh!" Holly placed a finger over her mouth.

"Right." Katie glanced left then right. "I have a break soon. We could ask around at other buildings where Daniel Croaker completed inspections. We could break into his office and read his files. A real cloak and dagger mission. Or, we could visit *The Pie Crust* and tease information from the Great Junie Bug. She might kick us out but it would be worth it."

Holly laughed. "If the chief and his top detective could hear us now."

"I know. It's great. So where should we start?"

"I know just the place! Let's go."

***

WHAT THEY WERE DOING wasn't really breaking any laws. It was perfectly justifiable, even if their boyfriends had been with them. They might not approve but that was a different matter.

"Tell me again how you got this information?" Katie sat in the passenger seat of Holly's car and stared at the ranch across the street.

"The phonebook." It wasn't a lie. Okay, maybe she first learned the address reading Detective Howe's notes, but she confirmed it with the white pages.

"Smart. So what's the plan?"

"Poke around and see what we can find. Maybe there's an unlocked window or something." Holly climbed out of the car. Katie met her on the street. "We'll act casual."

Together, the two strolled across the street. After a quick glance, Holly led them across the grass and to the back of the house. Her skin prickled but Holly blamed it on their mission. Why in the world would Howe pay a cop to follow her around? What a waste of taxpayers' money.

"I feel like I should be wearing black and a ski mask," Katie whispered.

"I think the neighbors would call the cops."

"Right."

They peeked in the windows, testing, to find them locked. At the back of the house, they crossed a patio and tried the back door.

It opened.

Katie gasped. "What? How is it unlocked?"

Should they enter? Was it really so wrong when the guy had been murdered? He had no known family. It wasn't like they were going to steal anything. "We could possibly be adopted sisters or concerned family friends here to visit."

"Definitely." Katie nodded, enthusiastically. "I'm great at cover stories." She paused, then said, "What exactly are we looking for? I mean, he's not the guilty one, he's the, um, dead one."

"I'm not sure exactly. He wasn't a kind man. Wasn't one to show mercy. Probably had little social life. No friends. But, if he'd been taking bribes to give false building inspections, even if it was only one, there might be a paper trail. A name jotted down on a piece of paper. A phone number." Holly pushed on the door, and they entered.

A musty smell, one of disuse, permeated the kitchen. Possibly, Croaker had lived on take-out food. For the most part, the place was clean. No stacks of dirty dishes or pots and pans. Holly tiptoed into the living room. Again, clean, and the feeling the guy didn't really consider the place home. She walked down the hall, Katie on her heels, and then into the bedroom. They poked around and peeked into drawers and trashcans.

"Nothing. Not even one clue!" Katie said, dismayed.

"Not obvious ones."

"What do you mean by that?"

Holly thought about single guys and how they lived. Of course, there could be exceptions to the stereotype. The man who's a slob and only rushes to pick up when a date arrives. This wasn't solid evidence, but….

"Talk to me." Katie nudged her.

"Most bachelors are slobs. Of course, not all, but most. This place is clean. Too clean. Almost as if it were picked up for a reason before he left. He could just be a type A germaphobe. The cops might've already been through here and cleaned out all the clues, which means we're too late. And that could very well be the case."

Katie beamed with excitement. "But you think it's something else."

"What if Daniel Croaker's house is the real murder scene?"

"Oh my gosh. Creepy but fascinating."

Holly walked back to the kitchen. "That would mean Croaker knew the killer. At least enough to let him into the house. There was no forced entry. Now, that could mean enemy or supposed friend or accomplice to his inspection scams. Did he work alone? In conjunction with any businesses?" She surveyed the clean table and countertops and the spotless sink. The dish drainer with clean plates and silverware. "What if this friend"—Holly made air quotes—"stopped by with dinner or dessert? It could've been a friendly meal, and Croaker completely clueless. Or, it could have been tense, the partnership fraying, or an enemy calling a truce, while—"

"I've got it," cried Katie. "While Croaker innocently partook of the gift of food, the killer snuck up behind him and strangled him."

"But there were no marks on Croaker's neck."

"Then…suffocated him with a pillow."

"Possibly," Holly said. "Or, slipped poison into the food and just waited, or returned later that night."

Katie studied the kitchen. "Of course, then the killer cleaned up every last crumb of evidence or connection to Croaker and deposited the body in the dumpster by your apartment."

"Then the killer got nervous and called in about the body, which is when Howe found me in the alley."

"Wow." Katie plopped down in the kitchen chair. "And we solved it because of a kitchen that was too clean."

"It's just a theory, and there aren't any legitimate suspects." Holly sighed. "Unfortunately, our boyfriends won't listen to us and we can't reveal we snooped around. They are the ones who have access to Daniel's phone records, bank and business accounts, his office files. Anything that would confirm our theory, or at least lead to the suspects."

Silence fell, and they sat, thinking. Holly spoke. "We should go."

"Yeah." Katie giggled. "Before we get caught."

They left the way they came. Holly made sure the back door was shut tight. They strolled back to the car and then made their getaway.

After dropping Katie off at the library, and heading home, Holly felt unsettled. Yes, the place had been too clean, and her theory was plausible. But a lot of the pieces were missing. Instinct told her that there was more to it. Right now, June Marsh certainly appeared guilty. Who else would want the bakery closed? Was it that simple?

14

Holly peeked out the window of her apartment. When Trent texted a couple hours ago and said he had time tonight for dinner she couldn't have been more thrilled. Her mind needed a rest from thinking about this case. She wished she could order a muffin at *The Pie Crust* and subtly ask June questions. Somehow, she didn't think that would come across well. The great one could kick her out forever. Holly didn't want a bad relationship with her future competition.

Someone beeped.

Holly looked out the window again. It was Trent! She twirled, allowing her black skirt to balloon about her legs. "How do I look, Muffins?"

Muffins just placed his head on his paw and flashed puppy-dog eyes. She rushed to him. She leaned over and gave him a quick cuddle. "I know you want to come, but this is for the best. I promise lots of walks and talks as soon as the craziness settles."

Trent beeped again.

"Okay, okay." She locked up and went downstairs. Ooh, he looked smart. Dark jeans and a solid red T-shirt. She whistled. "Hey, hot stuff."

He grinned. "You don't look so bad yourself." He opened the door for her and soon they were driving down Main Street. "Up for some Italian?"

"Yum! Sounds great." To be honest, Holly didn't care if they took a corner booth in a fast food restaurant and ate nothing but fries. She just wanted to spend time with Trent. Twice in two days seemed close to miraculous. She hated keeping her sleuthing activities from him. Yes, he would scold her, and she could take it, but she didn't want to stress him out while he worked at his new job. "So, how's the job going?"

He tapped his fingers on the wheel. "Pretty good."

"Seriously?" she asked. "That's all I get—pretty good? More details, Chief."

"You know I can't talk about the cases."

"I know but surely you can tell me how being a new chief of police is working out. Are you getting along with the cops? Do they respect you? Are you happy?"

He pulled into the restaurant and parked, then sat quietly. "As you know, the previous chief was a bad egg. The fact that for years the police department didn't know this has left them wary and suspicious. It's going to take time."

Holly got the distinct feeling that she was only hearing part of the truth. Maybe he wasn't being completely honest with how hard it was to be on the top. It could be a lonely place. Well, tonight would be about cheering him up and taking his mind off work. They entered the restaurant and found a corner booth. They ordered and were soon eating. She'd craved chicken Parmesan, and Trent, a meatball sub. On purpose, Holly chatted about everything except what was on her mind: *The Pie Crust*, June Marsh, Croaker, her theories, inspections, and perfect corpses with no obvious cause of death. She talked about meeting up with Katie and restarting a high school friendship. She talked about missing Charlene and Millicent and how she hoped *Just Cheesecake & More* was thriving.

Trent was strangely not as talkative as usual.

Eventually, her chatter dwindled, and she finished her dinner, her thoughts roaming back to the case. She could do nothing without knowing what the cops knew. Sadly, pondering the case was more exciting than planning for her future business. Her confidence had taken a hit.

Back in the car, Trent remained quiet. That was okay. She'd let him stew, be quiet. Their relationship was solid enough for that. Finally, he cleared his throat as if he had something to say.

"Yes?" Holly asked. "What is it?" She fake-punched him. "You going to tell me what's been bothering you all evening?"

"That obvious, huh?" He didn't say anything else. Holly waited, starting to seriously worry for the first time. Then he asked, "Any news on the business since we last talked?"

Holly didn't know how to answer. She'd told him about The Pie Crust and the suspicious rat plague, but she wasn't ready to admit her insecurities. That her experience in *The Pie Crust* had sucked the wind from her sails.

Something she wasn't used to experiencing. "I contacted a realtor earlier today, and I guess I wait for someone to call back. I fear it might be a wait. I haven't seen any available rental space where I want it."

"Hmm. I'm sure it'll happen. Do anything else today?"

Oh, darn it. He sounded suspicious. She caught a sideways peek, his face resolute, giving nothing away. "I spent time with Katie, you know, catching up. Making sure her boyfriend hadn't barred her from seeing me." She tacked on a laugh.

His silence and facial expression hit her hard and fast. A punch to the stomach. Hot prickles spread across her skin. Oh my gosh. He didn't need to say anything. It was obvious what he was thinking. And it wasn't that Holly was being silly or paranoid. More like it might, in fact, be good advice if Howe suggested Katie didn't hang out with her back-in-town friend.

He pulled up outside her apartment and sighed. "Detective Howe put a cop on Croaker's house."

"In case unknown relatives or family friends stopped by?"

"Yup."

Oh, crap. Of course, he did. Why wouldn't he? It made sense. Holly gripped the handle on the door. She wanted to say goodbye and end on a somewhat positive note—before it got worse. And, oh, it could get a lot worse.

"Funny thing. The report came in that two females were seen poking around. Peering in windows."

"Oh?" Holly's voice squeaked.

"Yes." He finally turned to face her, eyes piercing. "One had red hair."

"Hmm. Interesting." She felt the blood rushing to her face, her cheeks had to be blooming crimson. This was bad. She'd crossed a line with Trent, but she wasn't sure how this was any different from the other cases in Fairview. She couldn't help it if she stumbled upon a body in the dumpster. She couldn't help it if her mind worked at solving puzzles.

Something had changed. And she knew exactly what—or more like who—it was. "This has something to do with Detective Howe, doesn't it?"

Trent appeared flustered at her accusation, which also revealed it was accurate.

"That's okay. I get it. Honestly. He didn't like me from the start." She hadn't realized that Howe would go so far as to poison Trent's mind against her. "Did you even once question his accusations against me?"

"He didn't like you because you stuck your nose in a high-profile case. And I'm not even going to respond to the last question."

"I discovered the body and made a few observations. What was I supposed to do?" Holly wanted to throw on the brakes, send this conversation to a screeching halt before it caused major damage. But it was unstoppable, careening forward to the inevitable.

"I don't know." He hit the wheel. "Act like a normal person, maybe?"

For the second time, his words pierced her heart, carefully placed arrows meant to hurt. This wasn't the Trent she knew. It had to be job stress. Had to be. She opened the door. "I think we should say good night. Thank you for the dinner."

Even as she climbed out of the car and shut the door, she couldn't believe this was happening. She wanted to rewind everything and start over. She wanted to cancel the date and hold off this terrible squeezing in her chest. Instead of heading straight to her apartment, she strode down the street, needing to clear her mind and walk it off. She didn't look back even though she wanted to. Maybe Trent would call her name any second, apologize, or at least explain why he was so mad.

It didn't happen.

Gosh, they were reasonable people. Their worst fight had been nothing compared to this short and painful one. And he didn't even say everything he was thinking. From his silence, to his stony expression, Holly knew one thing. He was furious.

But why?

Was there more to the case than she realized? Had they truly been in danger this afternoon at Croaker's house?

She turned and walked back. So far, time in her new home had been one disaster after another. She hadn't even had a chance to tell him how deeply her fears and discouragement had affected her. He just assumed she had put that off so she could play detective. He didn't say the exact words, but he thought them. A suffocating feeling of dread fell over her. This wouldn't be fixed with a goodnight's sleep.

At her apartment, she stopped. Noise came from inside. Quietly, she pressed her ear to the door and heard shuffling and whispering. Her heart rate spiked.

She opened the door.

15

"Surprise!" Charlene and Millicent shouted.

Holly stumbled inside and into the arms of her dearest friends. Tears rushed to her eyes, and she felt shaky. She'd missed her friends but she hadn't realized how much until they were standing in front of her. It had only been five days.

Millicent, as usual, was dressed to the hilt, ready for a date with a movie star. White capris, aqua blue tank, and a matching headband held back her blonde hair. Charlene, also, was the same. Graying frizzy hair floated about her face. She wore khaki shorts and a shirt that was probably twenty years old that she'd worn working in her garden earlier that day.

"We know you had dinner with Trent, but we figured you wouldn't be able to resist some mini cheesecakes." Millicent laughed. "Yes, they're leftover from today, but who cares. Right?"

"Exactly!" Holly forced enthusiasm, approached the table, and loaded a paper plate, even though the thought of eating cheesecake turned her stomach. Yes, she was glad to see her friends, but really, she wanted to curl up on her bed, snuggle with Muffins, and either cry or get lost in a movie. Or both. She definitely didn't want to burden her friends, especially Trent's mother, with her problems. Because they were all connected, or seemed to be.

Holly plastered on a smile. She'd get through the next couple of hours, regardless. "Tell me everything." She turned to Millicent. "How's the shop doing?"

"Wonderful. Cheesecakes and pastries are flying off the shelf. Max is a fantastic worker. I don't know where you found him, but he's great. He does everything. It's nice to be able to focus on the business sometimes and not do all the baking. I mean I definitely put in the time, but"—she sniffed—"part of my job is creating new tasty treats." She rambled about customers and new ideas.

Holly zoned in and out, trying her best to pay attention. It was hard. Charlene studied her with a knowing look. Holly forced an even bigger smile. Charlene was too smart and knew her too well not to notice.

Millicent nudged her. "So?"

"What?" Holly had missed the question.

"When's the big opening day? Because we want to make sure we're free to visit the new specialty cheesecake shop even if it is an hour away."

Exciting news like the perfect rental space would've been good. "Well…"

"Give her a break," Charlene shot out. "It hasn't even been a week."

"Yes, but as we know life just falls perfectly in place for Holly Hart." Millicent turned to Holly. "Okay, so maybe there hasn't been enough time to establish an opening date but you must have some news."

"Not really. I'm still waiting for the realtor to contact me." Holly picked up a cheesecake, suddenly finding it tantalizing, and nibbled.

Charlene grunted, clearly unhappy. "Where's Trent? He was the one who called us. Figured he'd at least pop in and say hello."

"That's right. Has a wedding date been set?" Millicent gushed. "I'm a terrific event planner so I'm happy to help."

Holly didn't answer but studied her plate. Her friends' questions made it more than clear that her first five days could've been very different. She choked on her answer. "Work has been busy with Trent now being the chief…settling in, pleasing everyone…and what with the last chief being rotten, Trent's had to work hard at earning trust…um…he was exhausted…still had work to do…no time to plan anything…" There wasn't much else to say without the dam breaking.

Her friends were quiet. Holly couldn't look at them without giving it all away.

"Oh. My. God." Millicent gasped. "Do we need to sit that boy down and explain how this works?"

"I'm sure we'll get to planning." Holly hated that her voice shook, the emotion welling in her throat. She couldn't finish the thought—that Trent was working on a big case. Muffins left his perch by the window and sat by her feet, whining.

Millicent paced. "Let's march down to the station tomorrow and—"

"For being a journalist and supposed detective you sure can be stupid," Charlene snapped.

"What?" Millicent said, confusion obvious. "What did I miss?"

Holly didn't look but placed her plate on the floor and pulled Muffins into her lap.

Charlene hissed, "Something's wrong."

"What?" Millicent whispered. "Did I say something wrong? Because I promised in the car ride here, I would be all sugar and spice and everything nice."

They whispered back and forth. Finally, Holly looked at her friends. "I'm right here you know."

Charlene leaned into the couch. "Should we leave? Or are you going to tell us what's wrong?"

"Fine." Holly didn't mind telling them but she didn't know where to start. So much had gone wrong. Tears brimmed over, spilling down her face. Everything came rushing out. "This town hates me…new detective hates me and is poisoning Trent's mind…discovered a body…I'm a horrible pastry chef and I don't know why I thought I could make it in a bigger area…the Great Junie Bug will crush me like a bug… and…and…"

She couldn't admit the most painful part. Her fight with Trent. She could barely admit it to herself that his words had penetrated deep. It hadn't been a normal fight where he was just grumpy or over-tired. No, his issues had been about who she was as a person. And that she couldn't change. Never mind the trust issues. Whatever Detective Howe had said about her, Trent had let it influence him instead of sticking up for her or talking to her about it.

Her friends stared at her, mouths open.

Charlene truly was a terrific friend. She knew when to be tough and when to soften up. She knew when someone was being a spoiled brat and when they were truly hurting. "Whoa. That was a lot of information. Slow down and start from the beginning."

"Yes, tell us everything." Millicent leaned forward, her reporter senses finally kicking in. "Reinforcements are here."

Holly took a deep breath. She thought back on everything. Might as well go in order. "If you hadn't noticed, I live across the street from a bakery, *The Pie Crust*."

From there she told them all about the Great Junie Bug and the best cheesecake she'd ever tasted. That led to Daniel Croaker and how the previous bakery had been shut down through a smear campaign and possibly a falsified building inspection. Finding Daniel Croaker's body in the dumpster and how it wasn't connected to the big serial murder case Trent was working on day and night. Her run-in with Detective Howe and his immediate dislike toward her and the way he treated her during the interrogation. Everything spilled out. When she finished, she blinked through the fading tears. "So that about sums up my first five days here."

Millicent snorted. "Leave it to you to be solving a murder case so soon. Not surprising at all. I could tell the second I walked through the door there was a mystery afoot."

"Of course you did." Charlene winked at Holly. "We might as well call and book a few nights at a motel."

"Definitely. Max just asked for more hours. And I know my dad and Kitty and Ann won't mind helping. I'll call now." Millicent went down the hall to place her calls.

As soon as she was out of earshot, Charlene spoke. "How badly has my son screwed up? Do I need to give him a good scolding?"

Holly didn't know whether to laugh or cry. "Is it that obvious?"

"Yes. And Trent was supposed to join us. He planned the whole thing, including taking you out to dinner and meeting us back here."

"That sounds like Trent, but I assume this was planned last week?"

Charlene nodded.

"Let's just say a lot has changed in our relationship since I arrived." Holly's words came out a whisper. "We just had a big fight. One I'm not sure can be repaired with a couple words."

Wisdom and understanding emanated from Charlene. "Love has its ups and downs. If it's meant to be, if you're both willing to fight hard enough, it'll work."

Millicent entered. "What did I miss? I missed something. I can tell."

"We were just talking about a plan of attack," Charlene covered. "We'll take tonight to think about it and then form a plan tomorrow."

"I love it!" Millicent pumped her fist in the air. "Tomorrow morning? We visit *The Pie Crust*."

16

Holly bolted up in bed the next morning, confused and disorientated. It felt late, the sun slanting through her window in a different spot. She rubbed her eyes and memories from the previous day flooded back. With a groan, she flopped back onto the bed and whipped the covers over her head. She should be excited about investigating with her friends. She should be filled with dread about revisiting *The Pie Crust* and seeing their shocked reaction to June Marsh. She should be out in the kitchen, preparing a quick breakfast for her friends who would be by in a minute, and then making plans.

But she couldn't.

Trent's words, his facial expression, and lack of emotion toward her were seared on her heart. She meant what she said to Charlene the night before. This was one fight that wouldn't go away after a good night's sleep. She was glad Millicent hadn't heard. How would she respond? Happy that Trent might soon be free? Or happy in a vengeful sort of way?

They knocked on the door. Had to be them. It certainly wouldn't be Trent. Of course, she quickly brushed her hair and teeth before opening the door. "Coming!"

Millicent swayed into the room like a movie star.

Holly bit her lip, trying not to laugh. "Are those…gauchos?" Holly knew them as a style from the 80s. They were like capris but loose fitting and flared at the knees. It almost looked like a skirt.

"They're an upcoming trend. I promise." She sniffed. "I want to look my best when we go next door. It's like armor, to tell the truth. The more dressed up I am, the more confident I feel, the less her insults will bother me." Millicent's gaze swept the room. "What are we eating—cornflakes?"

"Sorry. I just woke up." Holly tried to smooth her hair once more.

"Get dressed," Charlene ordered. "The line's already too long for my liking. We'll fill up next door."

Holly rushed back to her room and dressed in jean shorts and a peach tank top. With Millicent's advice ringing in her ears, she applied makeup to hide the dark circles. Then added eyeliner and a sparkly lip-gloss. Might as well appear happy.

They stood in line ten minutes before approaching the doorway of *The Pie Crust*.

"Just give us a hint," Millicent begged. "I need to know something."

Holly shrugged. Now she understood why no one told her anything. The Great Junie Bug experience really wasn't something you could put into words. "Patience is a virtue."

"Whatever," Millicent muttered.

Two minutes later, they entered the shop. Holly stifled a laugh as she watched her friends observe the store and the people. Millicent's eyes widened to the size of saucers and she didn't even blink. Charlene took in the situation in her usual calm way.

June Marsh seemed to be in her prime. She slammed a fist against the counter. "What?" she roared. "You dare complain to the Great One?" The man at the counter trembled. If he spoke, Holly couldn't hear him. Millicent strained to hear. Seconds later, June spoke again. "Always finding the negatives about some thing or situation does not lead to happiness." Then, she shooed him away.

The man, grumbling and red in the face, stormed out of the shop. Everyone offered their two cents.

"Don't worry. You'll be back!" And…

"You're not alone!" And…

"Way to stick to your guns, man."

"Next!" June rasped out.

Millicent giggled and opened her mouth to most likely offer her opinion. "What—"

"Don't." Holly stopped her. "She'll know you said something bad about her. Just say nothing."

They moved forward, slowly, but were entertained the entire time. June Marsh sent one more person scuttling out of the shop in humiliation, and then, a few customers successfully ordered without too much drama.

Great, thought Holly. It was almost time for another scene, and they were up next. She whispered, "Speak loud enough but not too loud." She ordered. "Blueberry muffin, please. And a caramel latte. I'll pay for my friends."

June said nothing, her gaze narrowing in on Holly. She nodded while the paid help scurried in the background. Holly stepped to the side, a sigh of relief escaping.

"A skinny mocha latte and…" Millicent primped her hair while studying the showcase.

"You had plenty of time, blondie. Stop wasting my time."

Millicent quickly said, "A raspberry Danish." Then she said, "I couldn't help it if the line blocked the showcase. This is my first visit I'll have you know."

Holly wanted to kick Millicent for pushing her luck.

June huffed, and puffed out her cheeks like a blowfish. She shouted. "We've got a newbie, everyone!" The crowd cheered. June leaned over. "Maybe you should come back later when your ego isn't as large as me." She grabbed her stomach rolls.

Holly stepped in front of Millicent, pushing her to the side. "Charlene, what do you want?"

In a normal, calm voice, she ordered. "Oatmeal raisin muffin and tea." Then she added, "Please."

June nodded. Their orders arrived and Millicent and Charlene carried them to a corner table while Holly paid. Holly held her breath, waiting for some kind of insult.

"Come here." June motioned for Holly to lean closer. "I'll go easy today. Just make sure he's worth it." She handed Holly the receipt.

Holly startled.

"Oh, I can see past sparkly lip gunk." She winked. "How did you like the cheesecake?"

"Thank you to the Great Junie Bug."

Then June roared. "Who's next?"

And that was that. She was out from under June's watchful eyes. Holly found Charlene and Millicent. Somehow, Holly had the feeling that when June asked her about the cheesecake, she hadn't been looking for an answer. It was more like a pinprick, a tease. Again, she got the strange feeling that June Marsh knew all about her.

She sat at the table. "So?"

Millicent huffed. "I can't believe she's still in business. Rude. Insulting. I should give her a piece of my mind. If I was a reporter in this town, I'd make sure to write up an article showing exactly what I think."

Charlene sipped her tea, thoughtful. "I like her."

"What?" Holly couldn't believe it.

"She's an entertainer, and she's smart."

People in line mumbled and complained, the murmuring catching Holly's attention.

"Police! Let us through!"

Trent and Detective Howe pushed their way through the line. Their faces were grim but determined. Cuffs glinted from Howe's grip.

Holly lifted her latte to hide behind it. Cuffs? What was about to happen? They certainly weren't here to buy a cup of coffee, unless they didn't want to wait in line and had to rush to a stakeout.

"It's Trent!" Millicent waved. "Hey, Trent, over—"

"Shut up and let them work." Charlene couldn't take her eyes off the scene.

With firm strides, Trent and his top detective approached the front of line. "June Marsh?"

The woman paled beneath her painted-on makeup. For the first time, she seemed out of words. She nodded in affirmation.

"Well, that's a miracle," Millicent muttered.

Trent nodded at Detective Howe, who asked June to step out from around the counter. She squeezed through.

"June Marsh, you're under arrest for the murder of Daniel Croaker. Any thing you say can and will be held against you in a court of law." He continued with the spiel, and June didn't say a word or put up a fight.

The line of people pushed to the edges of the room, and the cops led her out and into the waiting police car.

"Wow." That was all Holly could say. How did they come to this conclusion so fast? There had been multiple and complicated facets to this case. It seemed a bit rushed to arrest someone so soon. Unless, proof had been found that Holly knew nothing about. She couldn't help but feel bad for June, humiliated in front of her customers and staff.

The hired help stepped up to take orders, and June's husband, Jay, appeared from the kitchen to help. But without June and after the excitement of the arrest, the crowd soon dwindled.

Millicent huffed. "Jeez. So much for delving into another investigation. We didn't get very far. What a disappointment."

"Oh, we're not even close to being done," Charlene stated, her eyes crinkling with insight. "We're just beginning."

"Explain?" Holly asked.

"Isn't it obvious?" Charlene waited, and when neither of them answered, she said, "June Marsh is innocent."

17

HOLLY, CHARLENE, AND Millicent huddled up in Holly's apartment. Every few minutes, Holly went back to the window, re-imagining the arrest, still in disbelief. She had always felt this case wasn't clear cut, that she'd been missing pieces, information, something that would shed light on it. Maybe the cops had found that missing piece? It wasn't like she could ask Trent or Detective Howe. Maybe Katie in a few days. But they needed that evidence now.

"Are you sure this has nothing to do with the serial murders?" Millicent sat hunched over her laptop, scanning the articles.

Still peering out the window, Holly answered, "It doesn't fit. The murderer called-in the body." Holly focused on that for a moment. "Which means, this person was insecure. They wanted to make sure the body was found. Is that because they wanted attention? They so wanted the body to be connected to the serial case that they mistakenly drew attention to it."

"That was pretty stupid," Charlene muttered. "If that's what they did."

Exactly, thought Holly, as she watched a hushed conversation happening across the street in front of *The Pie Crust*. Inspired, she turned to her friends. "Stay here. See if we've missed any shared information in recent newspaper articles. I'll be right back."

"Wait!" Millicent jerked her head up. "I want to come."

"Stop whining." Charlene leaned against the wall, arms folded, mischief in her eyes. "We have to work together."

"Fine," grumped Millicent. "Grab a notebook."

Holly watched as the conversation seemed to end. "I've got to go!" She rushed to the door.

"Don't forget the selfie stick!" Millicent cried, but Holly was already in the hall and flying down the steps.

Outside, Holly stopped and took in a deep breath. She didn't want to sound like she'd just run a marathon when casually asking a few questions. She strained to hear what was being said across the street.

Jay Marsh, usually subdued and grumpy, motioned in anger to a woman. Mousy graying brown hair hung limp around her face. Her plump figure suggested she'd visited *The Pie Crust* one time too many. Her body language radiated anger too. Finally, she raised her arms as if to say, I give up. "No way!" Then she stormed off.

Should she follow this mysterious woman—or talk to Jay, which had been her original intention? Before Jay could disappear back into the store or leave, Holly crossed the street. "Hey!" she called.

As before when she tried to talk to him outside of the apartment building when she first arrived in town, he ignored her. She walked straight up to him. If she wanted him to talk, she had to shock him. Nothing shallow. "I don't think your wife is guilty."

He paused, then finally turned, his gaze unfriendly. Holly could see it in his eyes—he was about to leave.

She started talking, the words rushing out as the thoughts formulated in her mind. She wasn't even sure if her thoughts were accurate, but she'd find out. "At least, she's not guilty of murder. The cops arrested the wrong person. Daniel Croaker was a building inspector. Your wife called in a few favors, pressuring or paying him to close down the competing bakery six months ago." She remembered Daniel storming out of the bakery, saying he'd been threatened. "Their business arrangement, at first, worked. Maybe Daniel was blackmailing June or the other way around. Either way, he needed to be eliminated."

"What?" Jay snarled. "That sure as heck makes June look guilty. Anyway, that man deserved to be done away with. But thanks." He sneered and turned away.

"Yes, but…" Holly bit her lip, then continued, "If Daniel Croaker was the kind of man to say yes to a bribe. Maybe he had before? Do the cops know this?"

"Just mind your own business, ya here?" Then he slunk into *The Pie Crust*.

Holly deflated. As she stared at the closed door to The Pie Crust, she got the distinct gut feeling that Jay wasn't telling the whole truth.

***

HOLLY FLUNG OPEN THE door and burst into her apartment. "June bribed Daniel Croaker to close down the competing bakery!" She deflated. "Well, maybe she bribed him." That's what she had wanted him to admit, but that would have been too easy. "I can say for sure that he definitely wasn't tell the whole truth."

Millicent laughed. "That went from something to nothing pretty fast."

"Of course, he didn't tell the truth," Charlene said. "It makes him or June guilty."

"If June was involved with a little bribery, there goes your theory of June's innocence." Millicent flashed a haughty look at Charlene.

Charlene stood straighter. "Bribery and murder are two very different things."

"Fine." Millicent huffed. "Then what are we missing?"

"Jay Marsh is not a very forthcoming man. I barely got him to say anything." Who was the woman Jay met outside *The Pie Crust*? A patron? Business owner? Lawyer? It could be anyone. "If only we had the name of the woman he was talking to."

"Ha!" Millicent blurted. "And you practically mocked my little detective kit at your going away party. While you were talking to Jay, I zoomed in and took the woman's photo."

"Okay…" Holly tried not to groan at the selfie stick.

"Using the selfie stick, of course." She plugged her phone into her laptop. "And now let's do a simple search by the photo and your town and see what comes up."

Millicent could've taken the photo without a selfie stick but Holly decided not to point that out. June seemed like a smart woman. Smart enough to know that murdering the man she had bribed would make her look extremely guilty. Especially if Daniel kept records or had anything prepared to send to the newspaper. If he had, the police had cleared the evidence from his home. She and Katie had checked. But if they had that evidence, they would've questioned or arrested June earlier. Still, she sensed she was missing something important. Maybe the cops were too.

"Aha! Here we go." Millicent turned the laptop so the screen faced Holly.

It was a newspaper article about women and business. The woman had a name. May Little. Holly's eyes widened. May, as the landlord, had stood in front of the very apartment building Holly visited the first day in town. And Jay Marsh had mowed the lawn.

"I'm going to pay May a visit." She might know something about Daniel Croaker. She might even know his business practices and be able to reveal whatever it was Holly was missing concerning Daniel Croaker's murder.

"What can we do?" Charlene asked.

"Visit the businesses and ask if anyone used Croaker for a building inspection. Just see what they say."

Millicent sniffed. "I have reporting skills. Maybe I should go with you."

Holly was about to argue, but Charlene agreed. "Yes. Go together. I'll canvas the local businesses."

"I'll grab the selfie stick," Millicent cried. "You never know."

18

"WHAT A DUMP," Millicent stated.

"It definitely needs some TLC." Holly couldn't argue her friend's observation. She'd thought the same thing last week.

"Pfft. More than that." Millicent rubbed the tips of her fingers together. "It needs someone with a lot of money."

They stayed in Holly's car for a moment studying the peeling paint and weedy lawn. Looked like Jay Marsh needed to work harder. It was easy to picture the building decades earlier with a shiny coat of paint, window boxes, and blooming flowers, rockers on the front porch, and maybe a large family living in the entire space. At some point, someone broke the old house into apartment units as an investment.

"If that's the truth"—Holly tapped the steering wheel—"then May Little is probably squeaking by without a lot of extra money to invest. As soon as something big like a new roof or new windows or furnace came along, she had to pay for those aspects, leaving little left for paint and lawn care."

"Which means, at some point, she did business with Daniel Croaker," Millicent stated the obvious.

Holly and Millicent approached the building. Just as they went to knock, the door opened and a young woman, about their age, exited.

"Hi, there. How are you?" Charm exuded from Millicent's every utterance.

The woman's gaze darted left and right. Definitely not expecting visitors. "I'm…fine. How are you?"

"Fine and dandy!" exclaimed Millicent. "Are you the landlord?"

A slight scowl crossed the woman's face. Not many would notice the subtle expression but Holly did. "No. May lives in the bottom right unit."

Breaking from script, Millicent motioned Holly inside. Her waving hands and wide eyes said *Go talk to May I've got this covered.*

As Holly walked into the building, she heard Millicent coax the woman into an extended conversation. "I hope you have just a tiny bit of time to spare. We're having the worst luck apartment hunting. We'd really like to talk to someone who lives and rents here before taking the plunge. And…"

The door shut quietly behind Holly.

She stood in the darkened hall. A musty smell permeated the air causing her nose to wrinkle. Nothing a good cleaning and new paint wouldn't fix. Millicent's guess about the lack of money was probably right. Or, May didn't want to invest and tucked the money away. A set of rickety stairs led to a hallway at the top. It branched to the left and right. On the first floor, there was a door to the left at the end of the hall, and one to the right. May's home.

Holly knocked on the door and waited. This could be a complete dead end. There had to be more than one inspector in town, but May also had connections with Jay Marsh. It would be interesting to see her reaction to the news of June's arrest.

Holly knocked again. The door pushed open under the force. "Hello?" She stepped into the room. "Is anyone home? I'm looking for a place to rent?"

A muffled voice answered, "Be right there!"

Time to put her observation skills to the test. Nothing in the cramped living room looked brand new, or even a couple of years old. The wear and tear and fading color on the loveseat and armchair screamed yard sale find. So, May was thrifty and didn't like to spend money. The end tables, coffee table, and mantle were littered with odds and ends. Everything from framed photos to figurines. So May was disorganized and sentimental or…plain old lazy. That could also attribute to the state of the building. There were no toys in the room, so no kids. No wedding pictures, so possibly no husband, at least as of now. Holly approached the mantle to study the photos.

"May I help you?"

Holly turned away. May Little looked exactly like she remembered. Middle-aged. Slightly round in appearance. Mousy graying hair. Holly wanted to suggest a trip to the salon but that was Millicent's department. "Yes, I'm looking to move to town. And I'll need a place to live. Just checking out places to rent." When May didn't respond right away,

Holly continued, "It's just me and my dog. I'm a good renter with references."

May smiled. The warmth didn't quite seem real. "I might have something for you."

It wasn't easy digging for information. Holly tried to find a roundabout way. "I'm also looking to start a business. The realtor should call any day." Holly acted worried, biting her little pinky nail. "I've heard through the gossip mill that some businesses have been closed down prematurely. Do you know anything about that?"

"Not really."

"Gosh"—Holly laughed—"I'd hate for a too-strict building inspector to shut me down my first month. Wouldn't that be horrible?"

"Yes, it would."

"I got a name. Croaker Inspections. Have you heard of it?" Holly winked. "Word-of-mouth recommendations are the best."

May didn't answer right away, then said, "I might've heard of the name."

"I know it has probably been awhile but have you done business with him?" Holly asked.

"No, I don't think so." She smiled sweetly. "But then again, my memory isn't what it used to be."

"Hmm." Holly straightened as if just remembering something and struck a finger in the air. "Oh, my. I just remembered. He's the one found in the dumpster last week. Everywhere I went people were talking about it."

May covered her mouth in surprise. "I hadn't heard. That's horrible."

Perfect. Just the invitation Holly needed. "Rumor says it might be part of that serial murder case. It's terrible. I was reading about it the other day. Quite fascinating. The killer leaves absolutely no clues at the crime scene. No DNA. Nothing. And the bodies? Clean as a whistle. Must be poison." Holly shuddered. "Creepy if you ask me." May glanced at her watch. Holly kept talking, lowering her voice. "I don't know if it's true, mind you. I heard that a few local businesses might've been bribing him to lie on inspections. Have you heard anything about that?"

May stiffened. "No, I haven't heard much."

May was lying. It wasn't shock but discomfort she portrayed at the supposed gossip. This told Holly that she knew about *The Pie Crust* and possibly knew Jay Marsh long enough to realize June had been one of the business owners doing the bribing.

"Jay Marsh works for you?"

"How'd you know that?" May's tone shifted from sweet to sharp. Then she calmed, and smoothed her shirt. "I'm surprised you know of him."

Whoa. Jay Marsh must be a sore spot. "I heard he was a potential handyman."

"Why do you need a handyman?" May asked, her eyes narrowed and the skin on her neck mottled with color.

"Don't worry. I won't steal your handyman. It's just that...did you know that June Marsh was arrested for the murder of Daniel Croaker? I was at *The Pie Crust* when the police barged in and cuffed her."

She clasped her hands behind her back. "I haven't read the news yet."

Once again, May seemed to pretend ignorance. That meant she was hiding something. Maybe her connection to June and Jay Marsh? But why? Some clue that would break open this case seemed just out of reach. "I'll tell you what." Holly leaned in conspiratorially. "I don't think June did it. June might have reason if she'd been bribing him to close down her competition, but why off him? Ya know? The trail leading back to her would be too obvious. No, I think the cops have it wrong. I think that other business owners were bribing him, too. And any one of them might have decided to tie off any loose ends." Holly paused, then asked, "How well do you know June?"

May's face had paled considerably. "I don't try to play sleuth but trust the police to do their work."

Holly's phone buzzed at her pocket. "Excuse me." Millicent had sent her a text.

Jay paid people in the building to lie to the paper about the closed bakery.

Holly had to read it twice. Question was: did May Little know about this? And was it important?

19

Given May's short and probably untrue answers, Holly shifted her approach. So far, she'd been beating around the bush. Maybe it was time to be more direct. She tucked her phone away, after reading the message one more time. May had moved toward the door to encourage Holly to leave.

Holly coughed and patted her throat. Then in her best stage performance, went into a full-on cough attack. Between gasps, she managed to say, "Hate it when this happens." More coughing. "Spit went down the wrong way." More coughing. She let it subside. "I'm parched. Is there…anyway you could zap…some water in the microwave. Maybe some…tea with honey?"

"Um, sure."

While May busied herself in the kitchen, Holly went back to the mantel and the dusty framed photos. One in particular was extremely interesting. Was this the missing piece? The info that connected everything? A plan formed. It was risky but worth it, even though it wouldn't help her relationship with Trent. She snapped a picture of the framed photo and sent it to Millicent, along with instructions. Then she sent Katie a text, hoping she was at the library and could respond quickly.

Then, her heart in her throat from the adrenaline mixing with fear, she faced May when she returned with the cup of tea. "Thank you so much." Holly accepted the cup and threw in another cough for good measure.

"You're welcome." May glanced at the door. "If you don't mind, I have an appointment. We'll—"

"Want to know what I think?" Holly didn't allow time for May to answer, because she knew it would be no. "I think this latest murder isn't connected to the serial case. Someone with an axe to grind killed Daniel Croaker and tried to make it look like the serial case. But whoever it was made one huge mistake."

A flush spread across May's cheeks, painting them crimson. "Wh-what's that?"

"They called in the murder. And that wasn't part of the serial killer's routine. Serial killers are very exact in their methods and usually don't vary from the program. But this killer wanted to make sure the body was found. Probably nervous. That was the mistake." Holly thought back on Daniel Croaker storming out of *The Pie Crust*, furious, and claiming he'd been threatened. She thought about the framed photo.

"We'll have to reschedule a time to show you the available unit." May stepped toward the door.

Holly moved in front of the door and confronted May. "June might not have killed Daniel Croaker but her husband, Jay Marsh, paid tenants in your building to lie to the paper. That wasn't the real travesty. Those lies were to validate Daniel's Croaker's fudged inspection report. A business owner had to close shop, unfairly."

"Time for you to leave!" May tried to shove Holly out the door.

Holly held her ground. *Come on, Katie. Don't let me down,* thought Holly, as she pushed back against May. "I also think Daniel grew tired of being harassed and teased by June. Knowing he had no leg to stand on as he'd be found for his sins, when he confronted her, June kicked him out of the bakery, promising to cut off the goods, probably humiliating him in front of the customers."

"I must ask you to leave, or I'll call the cops," May threatened.

Holly's phone buzzed. She had to read the message before she left, but first, she had to throw May for a loop, stun her for a second. "How did you feel about your sister's arrest?" Holly raised her voice. "Did you help her by killing Daniel Croaker?"

May gasped and stumbled back.

Holly whipped out her phone and read the message. Eureka! It was worse than she expected. She softened her voice. "But no, why would you do that? That would be way too generous. For you didn't really care for your sister or her manners. You let Jay talk to your tenants, but then…when you needed money to pay off Croaker so you could keep your apartment building which should be torn down, your sister refused."

A jolt seemed to zap May. She straightened, her fists clenching at her sides. Her gaze pierced Holly.

"It was just too easy to frame your sister, given her history with Croaker. Buy one of her pies, inject it with poison, and bring it as a peace offering to Daniel. Maybe you didn't mean to kill him. Maybe, it was meant to be a warning through food poisoning." Holly remembered the phone conversation she overhead in line at the grocery store. "In fact, you didn't have to deliver the pie. He had an appointment with you, here, for the final inspection. And you kindly offered him a slice. When he died, that's when you left him in the dumpster, hoping to get away with the murder." Thoughts formed while Holly was talking. This left her breathless. She wasn't sure she was exactly right, but she had to be close. Hopefully, everyone else had played their part.

It happened fast.

May grabbed a heavy and ugly lamp. With a guttural cry, she attacked Holly, the lamp aimed for her head.

Holly ducked, and the lamp crashed into the wall. It crumbled and plaster dust filled the air. Holly coughed and moved away, crouching, prepared for anything.

"How do you feel with your sister in jail for the crime? Happy? Or filled with regret? Would Jay have put the pieces together? Your time was limited at best, May. You might as well confess."

May screamed, her face red, and attacked again.

Someone blurred into the room, tackling May to the floor. It was Millicent. With May underneath, she waved the selfie stick in the air. "I got it all!" she cried.

Behind Millicent, Detective Howe stormed into the room. Except, instead of heading straight to May Little, he body-slammed Holly to the floor. The impact caused her to lose her breath. She gasped out a few unintelligible words.

"Save it," Detective Howe snarled. With a too-tight grip, he yanked her arms back, twisting them harder than necessary, then he slapped on the cuffs. "You have the right to remain silent. Anything you say can be held against you in a court of—"

"Detective Howe!"

A tear slipped from Holly's eyes. It was Trent. He would stop this madness.

Howe pulled Holly to her feet, and the cuffs dug into her wrists. She cried out. "Our plan worked perfectly, Chief. We brought in June as a decoy, and the real team of killers ended up fighting. Holly Hart has spent time researching at the library. She discovered Daniel Croaker's role in shutting down the competition and feared the owner of *The Pie Crust* would do that to her aspiring business plans. So she got rid of the biggest threat: the building inspector."

Trent wouldn't look at her. He stayed calm. "You have evidence to back this up?"

"I've had a cop on her since she discovered the body. She's been observing and stalking her competition, *The Pie Crust*. She broke into Daniel's house to hide any traces of her communication with him under the guise of playing amateur sleuth. She fabricated the phone conversation she overheard in order to make him look guilty, along with whoever called. By playing sleuth, and taking advantage of her history with you, she appeared innocent. The perfect crime."

Millicent stood to her feet. "That is the most ridiculous fantasy tale I've ever heard. And trust me, as an embellisher myself, even I wouldn't go that far."

Trent nodded. "We'll take them both. Work it out downtown. Look at all the evidence."

20

LATER THAT EVENING, Holly left the station, weary and discouraged. Her body was sore, and she felt like she'd spent a few rounds in the ring with a sumo wrestler. Not only from Detective Howe's body slam but her interrogation afterwards at the station. The experience had been grueling. Howe, under the careful watch of the chief, revealed photo after photo, backing up his theory.

That Holly was a killer.

That she murdered the building inspector before the papers could launch a smear campaign against her. It was ridiculous. Trent saw right through it. Holly let out an involuntary shudder. When Trent had pulled rank and stated that it was all circumstantial evidence, Howe's burning gaze aimed at her had been nothing but cold, naked hatred. She couldn't shake it.

The real evidence pointed to May Little. The fact that she and June Marsh were sisters. The fact that Daniel's schedule revealed that on the day of his death, he had an appointment to inspect May's building. The toxicology reports revealed poison. The best guess was through one of June's pies. That part didn't even matter. Millicent's videos, taken with the selfie stick, of all things, had helped. Even though May hadn't given a confession in the heat of the moment when Holly had presented her theories, her body language and reaction corroborated what Trent already suspected.

Howe had called him biased and weak and strode from the room.

With a sigh, Holly entered her apartment. Muffins yipped and ran up to her. Tears threatened. She scooped the adorable little dog into her arms and cuddled. Millicent put a glass of wine into her hand.

"Thank you." Holly sounded broken and tired.

Charlene leaned against the wall, arms folded, waiting. She said nothing as Holly flopped into the armchair and sipped her wine. Millicent wasn't quite as patient.

"Tell us everything. We're dying here. Why in the world did that awful man arrest you? Did he get written up for violence? You should press charges. Evil. Pure evil. Though, he was kinda cute but that's beside the point. Did Trent beat him up?"

"Millicent…" Charlene only had to say her name.

"Fine." She huffed. "Give her a chance. I know."

Holly stroked Muffins curled into a ball on her lap. She had to hold it together because she owed her friends some kind of explanation after their support in all this. "The video helped." She smiled at Millicent. "May's response to my accusation spoke volumes. Enough to keep her and question her. Sounded like they also suspected her and have evidence."

Millicent clapped. "So my work was the nail in the coffin."

"Definitely."

"Seriously, will that horrible man get fired?" Millicent asked.

Holly shook her head. "I don't think so. Supposedly, he's one of the best detectives in the area. Trent would never fire him. It would look bad. The guy already accused Trent of being biased toward me as a suspect."

"But his theory was nonsense," Charlene stated.

"Yes. Trent called it misguided but thoughtful. A little extreme but a way to think out of the box."

Millicent gasped. "He didn't defend you? I watched that Neanderthal body slam you. If Trent had seen it, he'd have been furious."

Holly couldn't answer at first. At least not that question. "He's trying really hard to earn the respect of the force. He can't appear soft or biased. And, he's working a stressful, ongoing case. The longer it remains unsolved, the more pressure he feels." Or that's what Holly had guessed. She understood but that didn't mean his words and actions, or lack of them, didn't squeeze on her heart.

"They have proof against May?" Charlene asked.

Holly explained everything the best she could. Just the facts. Everything she'd laid out to May.

"Wow." Millicent whistled. "Siblings. Jeez." She moved to the kitchen. "I know it's summer but we picked up some chicken noodle soup. Want some?"

"Yes. I'm starving!" Together, they sat at the table and ate dinner. Finished, Holly leaned back in her chair. "Thanks so much for helping with this and coming to my rescue. I couldn't have done it without our combined effort."

Charlene's eyes twinkled with mischief. "We wouldn't have missed it for anything."

"Terrific fodder for a mystery novel." Millicent rubbed her hands together.

Someone knocked on the door. "Holly?"

Holly tensed. It was Trent. And, of course, Charlene went to answer the door. Trent walked in to three somewhat tense and accusatory looks.

***

HE STOOD IN THE doorway, exhausted, and after seeing the reception, wary. His hair was mussed and the shadows under his eyes revealed he'd spent sleepless nights, if not at the station, then at home, reviewing the unsolved cases. An ache returned to Holly's heart. All she wanted to do was support him, hug him, hold him. The case weighed heavily on his mind and shoulders. That much was obvious, at least to her it was.

Charlene took charge before Millicent could spark an inquisition. More like a judge and jury. The guy would be hanged within ten minutes. "I've been here a couple days and haven't even had a hug from my son."

He smiled and moved forward into her arms. "Thanks, Mom," he said, softy.

Holly was torn. Did she forgive? Or hold him accountable for his hurtful words and actions? Was the stress of the case enough of an excuse? Frozen with indecision, she did and said nothing.

Charlene moved to grab her things. "We'll have to visit again. And next time, we're having breakfast, lunch, and dinner together before I leave."

He smiled. "It's a promise."

"What?" Millicent's look of bewilderment wasn't too hard to decipher.

"Time for us to leave," Charlene stated.

"I don't know about that," Millicent stuttered, then complied after Charlene's sharp look.

Charlene hugged Holly then stood at the door. "You can tell me about your new mystery novel on the ride home. I'll tell you what's good or not."

Millicent brightened. "Seriously?" With affirmation from Charlene, Millicent hugged Holly. She whispered, "Don't you dare let him get away with this."

Then they left.

The awkward silence in their wake was painful.

"Want something hot to drink—coffee or tea?" she asked.

"Coffee would be nice, thanks." He sat at the kitchen table while Holly made a pot. Soon, it was gurgling and the dark roast aroma scented the room.

Holly sat across from him and waited. Surely, he came here with something to say. She wasn't going to start the conversation, not when she didn't want to hear everything he came to say. She poured two mugs when the maker spit out the last few dribbles of coffee.

He sighed. "Because I know you're dying to know, and I feel I owe it to you, I thought I'd share the details of the case. It'll be out in the papers soon anyway."

"That would be nice." At this point she could care less about the case. What she wanted was to see the warmth and love back in his eyes. For him to reach across the table and hold her hand. Tell her everything was fine. Apologize. Then she could suggest scheduled date nights.

He traced the rim of the mug with his finger. "As you might've guessed, the details of this murder were kept from the papers and public. We wanted everyone to believe this was part of the serial case. June was arrested as a decoy, so our top suspect would relax."

"You mean me?"

"No," he said, his tone weary and worn down. "It was May Little."

"You figured out they were sisters."

"Yes. June had asked Daniel Croaker to be lenient with May and threatened to cut him off from all baked goods. That was what you witnessed before he was murdered."

"He also had grown tired of June's harassment every time he entered the bakery." Holly couldn't help herself. Maybe she wanted to prove something to him, earn his respect. Or maybe she wanted to delay any talk of their relationship. "The day he was murdered he had an appointment with May Little to inspect her apartment building. May, knowing her sister had bribed Croaker to shut down the competing bakery, had asked June for money so she could do the same. June refused. So, May asked her to pressure him into it. When that didn't work, May decided to teach Croaker a lesson. She injected some kind of poison into one of June's pies and offered it to Daniel when he arrived. Except...she didn't mean to kill him. Just warn him. Then, knowing about the serial murders, instead of framing June, she decided to make it look like one of the dumpster deaths. Did I miss anything?"

"No. That about covers it." Except, Trent wasn't impressed.

The fact that Holly knew so much about the case left him looking sad. What he didn't know was why Holly had delved into the case. Not only had she stumbled upon the body and had a detective add her to the suspect list, but the case had been tied in with the previous bakery closing. She'd been researching. But when boiled down, she supposed she could've stayed out of it. "I know you're mad."

"Mad? More like disappointed, frustrated." He paused, his grip on the mug tightening. "This isn't Fairview. You could've been seriously hurt. Why can't you just focus on your business?"

"I am." Holly still didn't feel up to confiding her fears to him. There was a wall separating them, and a part of her felt vulnerable and didn't want to share that with him while their relationship was tense.

"Detective Howe had been extremely loyal to the previous chief. His trust took a hit when all was revealed." His gaze, this time, was filled with honesty and concern. "He knows you were involved in taking him down."

That piece of news floored Holly. "Howe is a professional. A detective. Yes, I was involved, but I never held a gun to Chief Harrison's head and forced him to break the law."

Trent shrugged. "I know that. And somewhere deep down, Howe does too."

Somewhere deep down? "That doesn't sound very professional." She bit her lip. What a big mouth. She needed to keep her criticism to herself.

Clearly, Trent thought so too. He stiffened, then pushed back from the table. "Thanks for the coffee. I better get back to work."

"It's evening. Shouldn't you be able to head home?" Holly's question was more like an accusation.

He stopped at the door. "My job is serious work. Sorry that I can't take time to explore hobbies." He nodded. "I've got to go." Then he left.

Holly was flabbergasted. She headed to the window and watched him leave. There was a lot he'd left unsaid.

Probably because it wouldn't have been very nice. Muffins curled at her feet. She stared as the sun sank below the horizon, then she focused on *The Pie Crust*. "What am I doing to do, Muffins?"

That was the question.

So far, all her hopes and dreams for the big move had been crushed. More time with Trent and strengthening their relationship was dead in the water. Not only because of the murder but because of the hours Trent's job required. The realtor hadn't contacted her and opening day for her new shop felt years away. She let out a sigh and closed her eyes. Tomorrow was a new day.

Life could only get better. Right?

THE END

About the Author

Laura Pauling writes about spies, murder, and mystery. She is the author of the Holly Hart Cozy Mystery Series and loves the puzzle of a whodunnit and witty banter between characters. In her free time, she likes to read, walk, bike, snowshoe, and spend time with family or enjoy coffee with friends. She writes to entertain, experience a great story, explore issues of friendship and forgiveness, and...work in her jammies and slippers.

Visit Laura at http://laurapauling.com to sign up for her newsletter or send her a message through the contact tab. Or email her directly at laura@laurapauling.com.

Made in the USA
Monee, IL
04 March 2023